"It's my son's future, Daniel," Beth said quietly.

"So that weighs against me selling the store." She paused, seeming to consider her decision. "If it were just my concern, I'd turn the offer down."

Daniel nodded. That was only right. "Take your time, Beth. Talk to anyone you want. I'm not in any hurry. Whatever you decide, I won't argue."

"Denke." Relief flooded her face. "I don't want to be at odds with you. No more misunderstandings between us—it's much better to speak honestly, *yah*?"

Daniel immediately thought of his promise—of the thing he should tell her but couldn't. No. He corrected himself even as he had the thought. It wasn't he who should tell Beth. She seemed to take his agreement for granted, so he didn't have to speak.

An image of the life he really wanted arose in Daniel's mind—a picture of himself and Beth together, with Benjy growing up and working beside him. But given his secret, that now seemed very far away, if not impossible…

A lifetime spent in rural Pennsylvania and her Pennsylvania Dutch heritage led **Marta Perry** to write about the Plain People, who add so much richness to her home state. Marta has seen nearly sixty of her books published, with over six million books in print. She and her husband live in a centuries-old farmhouse in a central Pennsylvania valley. When she's not writing, she's reading, traveling, baking or enjoying her six beautiful grandchildren.

Books by Marta Perry

Love Inspired

Brides of Lost Creek

Second Chance Amish Bride
The Wedding Quilt Bride
The Promised Amish Bride
The Amish Widow's Heart

An Amish Family Christmas
"Heart of Christmas"
Amish Christmas Blessings
"The Midwife's Christmas Surprise"

Visit the Author Profile page at Harlequin.com for more titles.

The Amish Widow's Heart

Marta Perry

LOVE INSPIRED
INSPIRATIONAL ROMANCE

LOVE INSPIRED®
INSPIRATIONAL ROMANCE

PLEASE RECYCLE

THIS PRODUCT IS RECYCLABLE

Recycling programs
for this product may
not exist in your area.

ISBN-13: 978-1-335-48794-0

The Amish Widow's Heart

This edition published by arrangement with Harlequin Books S.A.

For questions and comments about the quality of this book,
please contact us at CustomerService@Harlequin.com.

Love Inspired
22 Adelaide St. West, 40th Floor
Toronto, Ontario M5H 4E3, Canada
www.Harlequin.com

Printed in U.S.A.

With all lowliness and meekness, with longsuffering, forbearing one another in love; Endeavouring to keep the unity of the Spirit in the bond of peace.
—*Ephesians* 4:2–3

This story is dedicated, as always,
to the love of my life, my husband, Brian.

Chapter One

Bethany Esch looked at her husband's black jackets, hanging from the wooden pegs on the bedroom wall, and her heart failed her. She took a hasty step backward, bumping into the large box her cousin Lydia was carrying, and fought the panic that filled her.

Lydia dropped the box onto the double bed, catching Bethany's arm when she would have fled from the room, her lively face sobering when she saw Bethany's expression.

"Beth?" Lydia shook her arm lightly. "Komm now. It's time we got busy."

"No, I can't. It's too soon."

Lydia knew her so well. Why didn't she see that Bethany couldn't get rid of James's clothes? Not yet.

"It's been over a month." Lydia hugged her as if to soften the words, but nothing could really ease them. James was gone.

"I know it's hard, but you'll feel better once it's done, and James's things will be a blessing to someone else."

The tears that came so easily filled Beth's eyes. "It doesn't feel like a month. It feels like yesterday."

She lived it again—the township police officer coming to the door late in the evening, his face somber, his voice halting as he described the accident: the Englisch driver going too fast on the narrow road, young and careless, unable to stop when he saw the buggy light.

"I know." Lydia's hand stroked her back in a comforting gesture. "The accident was such a shock. That makes it much worse. But…"

Beth wiped tears away with her fingers. Lydia was right, she supposed. James's death would be easier to face once she didn't have constant reminders. Easier for Benjy, too, and that was the force that strengthened her spine. At four, Benjy didn't understand, but he was beginning to accept the fact that Daadi wouldn't be coming home anymore.

She could hear him now, giggling at something her niece Janie had said. Fourteen and the child of Beth's oldest brother, Janie had been a treasure over the past month, showing up often to watch Benjy or take him to play with her little brothers and sister.

"Yah, okay." She straightened, trying to find a smile. "You're right. I certain sure can't let Benjamin see me falling apart."

"Gut." Lydia gave a brisk nod of approval. "The sooner we start, the sooner we're done. You hand things to me, and I'll fold and pack."

Taking the first jacket from its hook was the hardest. This was the jacket James wore for worship, and she'd always thought he looked so handsome in it, his fair hair even lighter against the black wool. She forced herself to hand it on quickly, resisting the urge to press it against her face.

Somehow, once she'd done the first one, the action became easier. She was helped along by Lydia's constant flow of chatter, talking about the latest news running through the Amish grapevine of Lost Creek—who was harvesting a big crop of celery, hinting at a wedding soon, how her daad's vegetable stand was doing now that fall was coming on, who had missed worship last Sunday and why. Lydia, with her lively personality and ready laugh, was a good antidote to pain.

"Did I tell you I have a letter from Miriam?" she said now. "She actually got it out quickly this time. I've already added my share, so you can do yours and put it in the mail."

"I'll try," she said, although writing a newsy letter felt like an impossible chore just now.

Miriam Stoltzfus, the third of their trio of cousins, had moved out to Ohio to stay with an aunt and uncle several months ago, and they both missed her. Their round-robin letters weren't a good substitute for seeing her.

The three of them had been closer than sisters since they were babies sleeping on their mammis' laps during worship, born within weeks of each other. Better than sisters, maybe, because they didn't have the rivalry some sisters did: Lydia, lively and mischievous; Miriam, quick and daring; and her, always trying to keep the other two out of trouble.

"You know what Grossmammi would say," Lydia said. "Don't try, just do it."

Beth actually did smile over that—Lydia had caught their grandmother's attitude perfectly. Grossmammi never shrank from any task, no matter how difficult. She had shrunk with age, and her memory might be a little misty, but nothing could quench her spirit. Would Beth ever reach that calm acceptance of what came?

With the hanging clothes packed away, Beth turned to the bureau. It was easier, she found, if she picked things up without concentrating too much on what they were and just passed them on to Lydia. The very act of doing something positive seemed to be lifting her spirits, making her pay attention to what was going on around her.

Family and church members had been in and out constantly for the past month, taking over so much that there'd been little she had to do. And Daniel, James's partner in the general store, had taken care of everything there. She was better for something to do.

At some point she had to talk to Daniel and make some decisions about the store, but not yet.

She reached for the last few items in the drawer, her fingers touching something that wasn't cloth. Paper crinkled under her fingers.

Curious, she pulled it out of the drawer to look at. A half sheet of paper, torn off and folded. Frowning, she flipped it open, read the few words it contained and felt her heart freeze.

Beth stared at the penciled words, trying to comprehend, but her brain felt as chilled as her heart. She forced herself to concentrate, reading the words as slowly as if they were in a language she barely knew.

I have to see you one more time. Meet me to-morrow night at the usual place. Please. Don't fail me.

There was no signature, only a penciled heart shape. No name. No date. But the meaning was clear, wasn't it?

"Beth? What's wrong? Tell me." Lydia's arms came around her, and she sounded almost frightened. Beth knew she must look terrible. As terrible as she felt.

"I can't." She stammered the words out and thrust the paper toward Lydia, glad to have it out of her hand. She clung to a faint hope that Lydia would see something different in the words…something that wouldn't shatter her heart and grind it to dust.

Lydia gasped, and then she was silent, probably trying to take it in as Beth had done.

"Maybe…" Lydia was hesitant, her blue eyes dark and troubled. "Maybe it doesn't mean what it seems to."

She didn't sound as if she believed that any more than Beth did.

"What else could it mean?" Anger and pain broke through the ice that encased her. "Someone…some woman…was meeting James on the sly. The usual place—what else could that mean?"

"Maybe…" Lydia faltered, clearly trying to think of some explanation that wouldn't hurt as much. "Well, maybe it was just someone who had a crush on James.

He was attractive, and he could be charming, but it didn't mean anything. You were the one he loved."

She clung to the words. That was true enough, she supposed. James's charm had been what had drawn her to him, back when they were teenagers. With his laughing eyes and his enticing smile, he'd had all the girls in a tizzy at one time or another. But he'd chosen her. He'd married her, promising to be faithful.

Something in her hardened against the pain and grief that threatened to envelop her. He'd promised to be faithful in front of God and the church.

"He was meeting this woman, whoever she was," she said firmly. She couldn't ignore the obvious. "That's not an old note—the pencil marks are still dark. Besides, I cleaned everything in this drawer not that long ago."

Her mind started to work again, remembering when that had been. Her gaze met Lydia's. "That was no more than a week before the accident. That note wasn't in the drawer then."

Lydia didn't speak. Most likely she couldn't think of another explanation, any more than Beth could. James had been seeing another woman just before he died. It was incredible. Impossible. But it had happened.

"That night," Beth murmured, almost speaking to herself. "He said he'd be working late in the store. What was he doing out on Owl Hollow Road? I never even thought about that…never questioned it."

"You think it was the night the note refers to?" Lydia understood her quickly. "But you can't be sure of that.

And you can't go around asking people." She sounded horrified at the thought.

"No, I can't go around asking." Pain forced the words out as she realized what this would mean for her. "I can only go on wearing black and pretending. No one must ever know, especially not Benjy."

No matter what she felt, she couldn't damage Benjy's memory of his daadi. No matter how much it cost her.

But there was one thing she could do. She could find out if Daniel knew where James had gone the night he was supposed to be working at the store. Daniel was James's best friend as well as his partner. If anyone knew James's secret, it was Daniel.

Daniel Miller turned from restocking the canned goods shelf to check the time. The plain round clock on the back wall of the store showed nearly four. Since they closed at five, business should be quiet for the next hour. Time for him to make the visit he'd been putting off for weeks—a visit to Bethany, James's widow.

He still couldn't get used to that word. *Widow.* They were too young to be experiencing this—it was for old people. If it affected him that way, how much harder must Beth be finding it?

Shaking off the question, he rounded the end of the shelves and approached the cash register, where Anna Fisher was taking advantage of their lack of customers to clean the glass-fronted cabinet.

"Anna?"

She glanced up, her round, youthful face responding. "Yah? Something you want me to do, Daniel?"

"Just keep an eye on things for me. I have to run an errand." He smiled, nodding toward the battery section, where his nephew Timothy was replacing batteries in their proper bins. "And you might take a look at those shelves when Timothy finishes. Just in case."

Anna nodded. Fourteen-year-old Timothy had been helping out for only a couple of weeks. They'd needed an extra pair of hands once James was gone.

Timothy was eager, but not always accurate. Still, Anna was responsible, not flighty like most sixteen-year-old girls, and she'd been working in the store for over a year.

"I'll manage everything. Don't worry." She was obviously pleased at being left in charge, but a trace of apprehension showed. "You'll be back to close up, yah?"

"For sure. No worries."

He headed for the door, pausing a moment outside to admire, as always, the General Store sign. They had a good location—he and James had decided the lot between their two properties at the end of Main Street would be just right for the business that was just a dream six years ago.

They'd surmounted plenty of obstacles on the way to making the dream a reality. He'd just never thought he'd be carrying on alone, without James. Pain clenched his heart. James had been his best friend since they'd entered first grade at Creekside Amish School together.

Funny, when he stopped to think about it, that they had linked up so quickly. He was one of seven, growing up on the ninety-acre farm that spread out from the road to the ridge that overlooked the village of Lost Creek. He sometimes felt lost in the midst of siblings, and it had been startling to realize that James's life was so different from his, even though they were part of the same church district.

James's mother was a widow, and James her only child. They lived right in town, and at six, James had known little of the farm life that was so routine for Daniel. But still, they'd been best friends, and when James married Bethany and they bought her great-uncle's holding and orchard, they became neighbors, as well.

The lane at the side of the store led back to Beth's property. Daniel strode along, noticing the signs of autumn beginning to show in the yellowing fields and the bright plumes of the sumac bushes. The leaves hadn't begun to turn yet, and the weather held sunny and warm, but the children were back in school and autumn was on the way. He could see the glint of red here and there in the apple orchard that covered the lower slopes beyond the farmhouse where Beth and little Benjamin now lived alone.

As usual, he felt a twinge at the thought of Beth. How would she manage without James? And just as important, what would she want to do about her share of the store?

He had his own ideas about that, that was for sure. He'd been Beth's friend even longer than he'd known James, since she'd spent a lot of time at her great-uncle's place. In fact, if she hadn't caught James's eye when she did, he might have been the one…

Well, there was no point in letting his thoughts stray in that direction. His task now was to do his best for Beth and her son.

As he neared the house, he caught sight of Benjy in the backyard, tossing a ball back and forth with Janie Stoltzfus, Beth's niece. Instead of heading for the back door, he veered to join them.

"Looks like a gut game. Can I play, too?"

"Catch the ball, Daniel," Benjy shouted, obviously pleased to have the game enlarged. With his silky straight blond hair and his round, chubby face, he still looked a little like the baby he'd been such a short time ago.

Would he have to grow up faster now that his daadi was gone? And at four, how much did Benjy actually realize about death? Daniel didn't have any answers, but he knew that Beth would do her best to protect him. And he would, as well. He owed it to his friend.

Benjy tossed the ball short of Daniel, and he had to sprint forward to catch it.

"Benjy's getting better all the time," Janie said, laughter in her eyes.

Nodding, Daniel sent a soft underhand toss in Benjy's direction. He put it right on target, and Benjy's gratified surprise at catching it made him smile.

"I got it. Did you see, Janie? I caught it."

"Yah, gut job," Janie responded. "Now throw it to me."

Benjy raised the ball to throw, dropped it and went

scrambling after it. Daniel took advantage of the moment. "Is your aunt Bethany inside? I need to see her."

"Yah. She was in the kitchen when we came out. Do you want me to go see?"

"That's all right. I'll find her." With a wave, he headed for the house. He tapped lightly on the screen door and went into the mudroom, then on into the kitchen, calling out as he did.

Beth answered, sounding normal, but when she turned from the stove and Daniel saw her face, he was shocked. During the visiting and the funeral after James's death, she'd seemed frozen, hardly aware of her surroundings. Now the ice that had encased her was gone, and he could read her loss too easily.

The gentleness had disappeared from her usually serene oval face, and her skin seemed shrunk against the bones, making her green eyes huge and tragic. Even her light brown hair had lost the curl she tried to suppress, straining back to the white kapp she wore.

He gathered his wits together and struggled to sound normal. "There's a ball game going on in the backyard. Don't you want to join it?"

Beth managed a smile at that, but it was a pitiful attempt. "Not just now. Can I do something for you, Daniel?"

"That's my question. You know I'm here to help with anything you want." He pulled out a chair from the kitchen table. "Can we sit down for a bit?"

After a moment's hesitation, she nodded, coming to sit in the chair he'd pulled out while he took the one facing it. "How…how is everything at the store?"

There was nothing of interest in her voice. In fact, it seemed that all her attention was turned inward to something that obsessed her to the exclusion of everything else.

"Doing fine." His voice sounded unnatural to him. "In fact, we need to talk about the store. I..." He stopped, shaking his head. "What's wrong, Beth? We're old friends, ain't so? You can talk to me."

A flash of something that might have been anger crossed her face and as quickly disappeared.

"Nothing." Her voice was tart. She pressed her lips together for a moment before continuing. "I'm sorry. You were saying, about the store?"

"Yah." He'd like to press the matter, because it seemed clear to him that even more was wrong than grief, but something told him it wouldn't be welcomed. She was only a couple of feet away across the width of the table, but it might as well be miles.

"I wanted you to know that I've brought my nephew Timothy in to help out, now that James..." He stopped and started again. "We needed a little extra help. Anna's a gut worker, but she's young and needs direction."

He took a breath, deciding he was going in the wrong direction. He didn't want to pile problems on Beth, only keep her up-to-date on the store that was her livelihood.

"Anyway, I thought you'd want to know what was going on. Business is gut, and naturally your share remains the same." He hesitated before going on with what he'd rehearsed saying.

"I thought you might want to be a little more involved now, since it's your business, too. You could come in a few hours now and then, maybe. Or look over the books, if you want."

She'd paid attention for a moment, but now he knew he'd lost her. She'd turned inward again, back to whatever it was that obsessed her. James's death? Tragic as that was, he sensed there was something more going on.

He'd thought to assure her that the store was under control and possibly to interest her in taking a more active role. But that seemed to be the last thing on her mind.

"Beth." He said her name gently, and after a moment her eyes focused on him. "It's all right. I'll keep on with the store the way I have been. I can see you don't want to talk about it now."

She nodded, putting one hand up to her forehead. "Not now," she echoed. "We'll talk later, yah?"

"Later." He stood, disappointed in himself that he hadn't found a way to help her. "Anything I can do, you know I will. I'll see you later, then."

But when he moved toward the door, Beth seemed to come back from wherever she'd been. "Daniel."

He turned, eager to do something—anything—she needed.

"There's something I need to ask you." She hesitated, as if trying to arrange her thoughts, and he waited.

"That last night…the night of the accident." She stopped, obviously struggling, but before he could say anything, she went on. "James said he was going to the store to do inventory."

Now it was Daniel's turn to collect his thoughts. Half-afraid of where she was going, he nodded. "Yah, that's right."

Beth had stood when he did, but now she leaned against the table, her hands planted on the top as if for support. She had always been slim as a young girl, despite having a child, but now she was almost gaunt.

"What took him away from the store? Why was he out on that road where the accident…"

She couldn't finish it, and he had a moment to compose himself. He should have realized that at some point she'd ask that question. He should have prepared an answer. Did she suspect… No, that was impossible.

Well, he couldn't lie to her, so maybe it was just as well he hadn't known where James had gone that night. "I'm sorry, Beth, but I don't know. We'd finished up, and he went outside ahead of me. I saw he had the buggy, but he was already driving out before I had a chance to say anything."

That was the exact truth. What he'd thought… feared, even…he would keep to himself.

"You don't know?" Her gaze was fixed on his face, her eyes enormous.

"I'm sorry." He sought for some possibility. "We'd been talking about adding a few more crafts to the store. Maybe he was going to talk to someone about it."

It sounded feeble, even to him. Why would James be doing that at eight o'clock in the evening?

But to his relief, Beth seemed satisfied. She nodded. Then, without a word, she turned back to the stove.

There was nothing more to say. He slipped out quietly.

It was all right, he assured himself. It had been a natural enough question for Beth to ask, once she'd gotten over the initial shock. There was no reason to think she suspected James of anything wrong.

He'd need to keep it that way. His loyalty to his friend, his deep longing to protect Beth and Benjy... everything combined to insist that whatever his suspicions, they should never be spoken.

By the time Mamm and Grossmammi arrived to take Janie home, Beth had managed to convince herself that she was calm. Unhappily, she was aware that her composure was like a thin sheet of ice, ready to shatter at the slightest breath. She forced a smile and went outside to greet her mother and grandmother. Grossmammi was already chatting with Janie and Benjy, which probably meant that she was having one of her good days, living in the present instead of the past.

"It's gut to see you, Grossmammi." She reached for the line to clip the harness to the hitching rail, but Janie got to it first. Benjy, very intent, helped her to latch it.

Her mother slid down, not waiting for a helping hand, and landed lightly on her feet. With her rosy cheeks and bright blue eyes, she didn't look like the mother of five.

They both reached up to help Grossmammi down.

She pressed her cheek against Beth's for a moment, but her attention was on her great-grandchildren.

"My, you two look as if you've been having a fine time. What have you been doing?"

"We played ball. Daniel did, too. And we gathered the eggs," Benjy said. "I found three."

"Gut job." Grossmammi patted his cheek. "How many did Janie find?"

It was apparent that number was beyond him, so Janie helped him out, whispering the number in his ear.

"Eight," he said proudly.

"We'll have scrambled eggs for breakfast, ain't so?" Bethany was pleased that she was able to sound almost normal. She glanced from her grandmother to her mother with a question in her face, but Mammi could only shrug, probably meaning it was hard to tell how long her grandmother would stay grounded.

Mammi lifted a basket down from under the buggy seat. "Who wants a whoopie pie?"

"Me, me!" Benjy bounced up and down, and Janie looked as if she would as well, if not for remembering that she was fourteen now.

"Let's go in and fetch a napkin, and then you two can have yours out on the porch while Mammi gets us grown-ups a cup of coffee."

Beth put an arm around her grandmother as they walked into the house together with Mammi following. It took only a few minutes to settle the kinder with juice and whoopie pies. Then the adults gathered at the table with their treat.

Grossmammi watched as she nibbled at the edge of

hers. "Better eat it," she said. "You've lost too much weight in the past month."

"Yah." She couldn't deny it, since the bodice of her dress hung loose on her. "I don't have much appetite."

"Natural enough," Mammi said. "But you must try. Take a real bite now."

Beth obeyed, inhaling the scent of chocolate and savoring the sweet, creamy filling. To her surprise, it actually went down without sticking in her throat.

Grossmammi watched her with satisfaction, her face alert. Mammi had noticed the alertness, too, because she relaxed a bit.

Her grandmother focused on Beth's face. "Now, tell us what has you upset today."

Beth narrowly escaped biting her tongue. How did Grossmammi know? Still, when she was alert, there was no getting away from her.

"Nothing," Beth said, hoping she sounded convincing. "I'm not upset."

"Ach, Bethany, tell that to someone who doesn't know you like we do." Her mother joined in. "Komm now, tell us. Benjy said that Daniel Miller had been here. Did that upset you?"

"No, no, of course not. He just wanted to let me know about how things are at the store." She hesitated. "Well, and talk about the future, but I... I wasn't ready to do that. He might have waited."

Mammi clucked her tongue. "That's natural enough for him, ain't so? After all, you are his partner now. He'll want to know how things are going to change."

"I suppose so." She felt a flicker of resentment.

She'd expected Mammi to be on her side. Not that there were any sides to it. She'd have to focus on business soon. Just not today. "Well, I can stop by the store sometime soon, but I don't know much about running it. James always said I had enough to do with the orchard and the garden and Benjy to look after."

"Yah, that's so." Mammi still studied her face. "You're sure there's nothing I can help with?"

First Daniel and now Mammi wanting to help. But they couldn't, even if she told them, and she didn't intend to do that.

"Nothing," she said firmly.

Mammi rose. "I won't tease you to tell me anything you'd rather not. Just remember we're here, and there are lots of people who love you and want to help."

Grossmammi reached out to touch Beth's cheek. Her grandmother had experienced loss, she knew, and Grossmammi's expression was tinged with sorrow as she looked at Beth. "And God is always ready to listen, ain't so?"

Beth managed a nod, tears stinging her eyes. She wasn't sure she even wanted to pray about this burden. Not now. Now she needed to be alone long enough to figure out how this had happened to her.

Chapter Two

Beth still had her grandmother's words in her mind a few days later when she and Benjy walked up to the orchard together. Grossmammi's advice was good, but Beth's prayers seemed to bounce around until she wasn't sure whether she was talking to the Lord or to herself. She prayed for acceptance, and in the next breath she was railing at James for his deception or wondering how she'd failed that he had turned away from her.

"Look, Mammi, look!" Benjy tugged her along, pointing. "Look at the red apples. Is it time to pick them?"

"Some of them." She steered him away from the McIntosh. They wouldn't be ready for a few more weeks. "Look at that tree. Those apples are called Honeycrisp. Some of them are ready to pick."

Running ahead, Benjy threw his arms around the tree in a hug. He looked up into the branches, standing on tiptoe to reach a ripe apple. "Can I pick it? Can I, Mammi?"

"Yah, for sure. Let me show you how." She closed

her hand over his small one. "Twist it just a little while you pull gently. Like this."

The apple came away in Benjy's hand, and he held it up with a delighted smile. "I did it."

Her heart swelled with love. "You did. See if you can reach some other ripe ones. I'll hold that one." She picked up the corners of her apron to form a make-shift basket.

Benjy darted off in search of others he could reach, and she picked a few more, inhaling the rich apple scent. It seemed to carry with it a score of memories—her little brothers vying to see how many they could pick, and Daniel, always kind, boosting the smaller ones up to reach.

Funny, that the orchard didn't carry memories of James. He hadn't been part of that early childhood, when Daniel as a near neighbor had naturally been there to help her uncle with the picking. James, living with his widowed mother in the center of town, had had no place there. Even after they bought Onkel Isaac's place, James had left the orchard to her.

So preoccupied was she with memories that she didn't notice the figure coming toward them until Benjy's shout.

"Grossdaadi!" He hurtled through the grass, his chubby legs churning, and bolted into her father's arms. Daadi lifted him over his head, then gave him a hug and set him down.

"Komm, schnell. See all the apples I picked. They're called Honey…" He looked at his mother.

"Honeycrisp," she prompted. "Because they're sweet

like honey and crisp when you bite into them." She polished one against her apron and handed it to him. "Try it."

Grinning, he bit into it, rewarded by a spurt of juice that dribbled down his chin. "Yummy." The word was muffled by apple, and she and Daad exchanged a smile.

When Benjy ran off to find some more to pick, her father gestured to the rough-hewn bench Onkel Isaac had built long ago. "Komm. Sit."

Once they were settled, he glanced around the orchard. "A gut crop of the Honeycrisps this year. You can sell some at the store, ain't so?"

Beth tensed at the mention of the store, conscious of the fact that she still hadn't had that talk with Daniel. "Did Mammi talk to you about me?"

He patted her hand. "You can't keep folks who love you from talking about you. You wouldn't want to, now would you?"

"I guess not," she admitted. "I suppose you think I ought to make some decisions about the store, too."

Her father paused for a moment, as if considering the matter. "You want some time, for sure. But maybe you're not seeing it from Daniel's point of view. With James gone, you own his share of the store. It's natural that Daniel would be anxious about your plans."

"I guess. But I don't have any plans, not yet." If she could be alone in her grief and betrayal...

"Sometimes I think Daniel is married to that store." Daad's craggy face softened in a smile. "It's natural, ain't so? He doesn't have a wife and kinder, and his father's farm will go to his brother. He's a hard worker. Always has been."

Was he making a contrast with James? She couldn't tell. "James did a gut job with the store," she said, feeling compelled to defend him, despite what she'd learned.

"Ach, yah, I'm not saying he didn't. All the more reason why Daniel wants to know what your plans are."

Daadi studied her face, maybe looking for a sign that she agreed. Then he glanced at the apples again.

"I'll send some of the family over tomorrow to help you do a first picking of apples. Then, if you want to sell them..." He waited, looking at her.

"Yah, all right." There was no getting out of it. "The Honeycrisp should be eaten when they're ready, since they aren't such gut keepers. We'll give some to the family." She forced herself to smile. "And I'll talk to Daniel about selling them."

"Gut." Daadi squeezed her hand, and that was as good as praise. "I can stay with Benjy while you go and see him. We'll go ahead and pick a basket for you to take to him."

She hadn't meant now, and she suspected Daad knew it. Still, if she must do it, it was better done now. And the same held true about making decisions for the future.

Daniel glanced up from the low shelf he was arranging at the sound of the bell and started to rise. He stopped for an instant before completing the movement. It wasn't his imagination. It was Beth.

He headed for her, relieved to think she was doing better. She must be, since she was here. Another step brought him close enough to chase that idea away. If anything, Beth looked even worse than she had the day he'd stopped by to see her. Strain had drawn her skin tautly against the bones of her face, and her cheeks seemed hollow. It was like seeing her when she was very old, and he could hardly keep from exclaiming at the sight.

For a moment he couldn't speak. Realizing that every customer in the store seemed similarly affected, he forced himself to say her name. "Beth, wilkom. I'm wonderful glad you came by today."

With a quick movement, Beth thrust the basket she carried at him. "Honeycrisp apples," she said, as if that was an explanation for her presence.

He saw the movement of her neck when she swallowed, and then she went on.

"We're going to do the first picking of the early apples tomorrow. Do you want a few baskets to sell? If you think anyone will want them, I mean."

"I'm certain folks will—"

An Englisch customer moved closer to peer at the basket. "Honeycrisp, did you say? I can hardly ever find them. I'll stop by on Friday morning. Hold a peck for me, will you?"

"Yah, I'll be glad to, Mrs. Warren."

"Good." She darted a curious glance at Beth before moving on to look at the bread case.

"There's your answer, ain't so?" Daniel smiled. "If you need any more help to pick, I can send my nephew over."

"Denke, but my daad is coming with some of the young ones."

"Your daad will get the job done fast. I remember what he was like when we all helped your onkel to do it. He's not one to take excuses."

She actually tried to smile at that. "He's still the same. He's watching Benjy right now so I could come over."

"Whether you wanted to or not," he finished for her.

"You did say we needed to talk about the store, ain't so?"

He touched her arm lightly and gestured. "Let's go to the back room. There should be coffee on." He raised his voice. "Anna?"

Anna Fisher, their sixteen-year-old clerk, sidled in from the storeroom and stopped. Shy, he supposed, at the sight of the new widow. Like everyone, she'd been shocked by James's death.

"Take charge for a few minutes. We'll be in the back, talking."

She nodded, moving behind the counter without wasting a word. He'd been doubtful at first that someone so shy would be successful as a clerk, but she'd surprised him. He was thankful for her now, with James no longer here to help.

Leading the way, he took Beth to the room that served as a combination office and break room. Sure enough, there was coffee staying warm on the small gas stove. While he got out cups and spoons, his mind worked busily, trying to figure out the best approach to this conversation. If he had his way, Beth would come in as a partner, and together they'd keep the store going as it was. But that might not be Beth's idea of a future.

He turned to the table, sitting down across from her as he put the coffee mugs in place. "How are you, Bethy?" The childhood nickname had come up without his thinking about it, but it actually made her face lighten a little.

"All right, I guess." But then her expression closed down again, negating her words. It made him want to grasp her hand, the way he'd have done when they were children and something had frightened her.

But he couldn't, of course. They were grown-ups now, and Beth was the widow of his best friend. He would help her in any way he could while still respecting her position.

Daniel cleared his throat, trying to find the way forward. "I... I hoped you might have made some decision about the store."

"Daadi said something about that, too." Beth ran her hand across her forehead, as if brushing away cobwebs. "I'm being stupid, I guess. James never talked about business with me. I don't even know how I stand and whether I have enough to support my son."

The thread of what might be anger in her voice startled him. He'd never heard her say anything critical about James. He must be mistaken. Beth had always adored James.

He'd have to assure her as best he could. "You needn't worry about supporting Benjy. You own half the business now, and we're doing pretty well. And you own the house and the orchard free and clear, ain't so?"

She nodded, her expression easing. "Yah, you're right. Onkel Isaac made it easy for us to buy. He was wonderful gut to me."

"Your uncle was a fine man, and a gut neighbor, as well." Little Beth had been his favorite among his many nieces and nephews, so it wasn't surprising that he'd wanted to protect her. "You want to stay where you are, then?"

"Yah, for sure. I never thought of anything else." She glanced up at him, a question in her green eyes. "As for the store…well, what else can we do but carry on as we are?"

It was tempting just to agree, but Beth ought to consider her options before she came to a decision.

"You do have other choices. If we go ahead as we are, we might have to hire another helper. Or you could come in and help. Even a few hours a week might be enough." He took a breath. "Or you might want to sell your share of the store."

There, it was out. If she did want to sell, he'd have no choice but to make the best of it.

"Sell?" She'd obviously never considered it. "Do you mean you want to buy my share?"

"No." Daniel couldn't get the word out fast enough, and it startled him. He hadn't realized he felt so strongly about it. "I mean, I'm afraid I couldn't afford it, not yet, anyway. But even if I could…" He struggled to articulate what he felt about the store.

"James and I took a risk when we started this place, but it's paid off. We liked working together. I guess now I'd like to think of Benjy growing up and becoming my partner, working beside me." He seemed to see the boy grown up, with his mother's sweetness and loving heart as well as his father's laughter and charm. "The store is his legacy from his father, ain't so?"

At his words, an expression he couldn't begin to interpret crossed Beth's face. He'd known her most of their lives, but he'd never seen her look like that before.

It was gone again, leaving him feeling disturbed without knowing why. "What do you think?"

Beth was silent for a moment, her gaze seeming fixed on something he couldn't see. Then she let out a long breath. "For now, I'd like to go on the way we are. But maybe that's not fair to you. James isn't here to do his share of the work, so we can't take his share of the profits. It wouldn't be right."

He hadn't expected that, and maybe he should have. Beth, for all her softness, had a strong sense of what was right.

"We can work that out," he said. "Like I said, we could hire someone else. Or you might want to spend some time helping out, ain't so?"

He could see how that idea shook her, could anticipate the instant refusal coming.

"I… I can't. I've never done anything like that. And anyway, I can't leave Benjy."

Again, he had that longing to reach out and take her hand. "Not full-time, no. But why don't you come in for a few hours a day? You can bring Benjy with you. He'd enjoy it."

"I don't know…"

He sensed her considering it and pressed his advantage. "It makes sense, Beth. You ought to see the operation for yourself. Maybe look over the books and get a little understanding of how it works. It's part yours now, yah?"

She rose, and he stood up with her. It looked as if she'd leave without a decision, but then she nodded. "I can't promise more, but I'll come in one day. Not tomorrow, but soon."

He'd have to be content with that for now. But he for sure wanted to know what was behind her reluctance.

The next afternoon Beth stood in the driveway, waving as her father's horse-drawn wagon reached the main road and turned in at the store. The apple-picking had been enjoyed by all the young cousins. She'd been expecting someone to fall out of a tree, but Daad had kept a stern eye on his grandchildren, so there'd been no horseplay.

Each of them had taken a small basket home with them. They'd stopped at the store to deliver ten peck baskets of apples. There'd be more in a few days, but she'd wait to see how the first ones sold. She didn't want to burden Daniel with anything he couldn't sell.

She was starting toward the back door when she saw a buggy turn into the drive. Company for her? She gave her skirt a quick shake, hoping she didn't have any leaves or twigs caught in her clothes. Then she recognized Lydia, so she smiled and waved, walking to the driveway to meet her cousin.

"How nice. I'm having lots of company today." She fastened the line to the hitching post. "Wilkom, Lydia."

Lydia gave her a quick hug and stood back for a moment, scanning her face. She gave an approving nod. "You look better today. Gut!"

"Always better for seeing you." They linked arms as they walked into the house. "Tea or coffee?" She usually preferred tea in the afternoon, but sometimes Lydia liked coffee. "I have a pot I made for Daad."

"Coffee, then." She took the chair she usually sat in for their afternoon break. "I saw your daad at the store. Looked as if they were unloading apples."

"Yah, we did the first picking of the early apples. I'll put some in a basket for you to take home. Tell your mamm they're Honeycrisp."

"I'll do that. Denke." She took the mug of coffee Beth handed her. "All right, tell me. Why *are* you looking better today?"

Beth shrugged, taking her seat. "I'm not sure. Just being busier helps, I guess. The apple-picking today, and yesterday I went to the store to talk to Daniel." She frowned a little at the thought of what she'd promised. "What about you? Have you been working a lot?"

Lydia nodded, making a face. "Waitressing at the coffee shop isn't a very challenging job. Sometimes I wish the regulars would order something different, just for a change."

"Why should they? You have the same thing every day for breakfast at home, don't you?"

"That's different. I have whatever Mamm cooks. If I had my way, I'd fix something different every day."

Beth couldn't help but smile. Lydia always claimed

to long for something different, but she went on in the usual Amish routine all the same.

"Laughing at me?" Lydia said. "Ach, I deserve it. I should be ashamed to complain. Never mind that, anyway. Tell me what Daniel wanted."

Now it was her turn to grimace. "Everyone keeps pushing me to make some decisions about the store, and I can't think of anything but…well, you know."

"Yah, I know." Lydia reached across the table to clasp her hand. "Did anything new come to light?"

"No. I asked Daniel where James was going that last night, but he didn't know."

"You think he was meeting that woman, whoever she was? It might not be that at all."

"Then what was he doing out on Owl Hollow Road?"

Lydia didn't have an answer to that. After a moment she countered with another question. "What exactly did Daniel say?"

She rubbed the tense muscles in the back of her neck. "He said they'd been working on something in the store, and when they were about finished, James went out first. I guess he thought James was just going home."

"So James didn't say anything to him."

Was there doubt in Lydia's voice? She couldn't be sure. But Daniel wouldn't lie to her. "If he'd known where James was going, he'd have told me." She clenched her teaspoon so hard her fingers stung. "Now I'm supposed to take over our share of the store, and I don't know a thing about it."

Lydia glanced down at the liquid in her mug, as if mulling something over. "I was always a little surprised that you didn't help out in the store sometimes, especially once Benjy wasn't a baby anymore."

"That's the way James wanted it. He said I had enough to do with Benjy, the house, the garden and the orchard. I never questioned it."

She'd grown so used to the fact that she'd never really wondered about it. Plenty of women with families helped out in the family business.

"It would be easier now if you had been more involved, but I don't suppose James envisioned a time when he wouldn't be there." Lydia glanced at her, as if to be sure her words hadn't hurt.

"Yah, it would be. I don't believe James ever considered the need. After all, his mother never did work outside the home, and she just had the one child and the little house in town."

Lydia's dimples showed at the mention of Beth's mother-in-law. "It's certain sure Sarah Esch never thought of anything on her own. I've never seen a woman so…so passive in my life."

Beth had to suppress a smile. "Sarah is like a soft, fluffy pillow you can push into any shape." Fearing that sounded critical, she hurried on. "But she's a wonderful, sweet mother-in-law."

"I guess." She hesitated. "Pillows are all very well to rest on, but they don't help you get anything done. And she always doted on James. Spoiled him, some folks say."

"He was all she had." Beth felt compelled to defend her mother-in-law, but it was true that Sarah's fluttering over James and then over Benjy drove her wild sometimes. "She's another person who can never know the truth."

"I guess not. But I just wish you didn't have to carry this burden all alone."

"I have you," Beth said softly. "Denke."

Lydia wiped her eyes and then chuckled. "We'd best find something else to talk about before we're both crying. So what are you going to do about the store now?"

"Daniel has this idea that I should start going in for a few hours a day. That way at least I can learn something about the business, but—"

"But what? It sounds like a gut idea to me," Lydia said. "Unless you're thinking to sell your share?"

"Daniel said something about the store being Benjy's legacy from his father, and it's true. If I sell, we'd have the money, but money isn't everything. Benjy wouldn't have the store."

"You don't have to decide right away, do you? Why not try Daniel's suggestion?" Lydia was practical, as always. "Maybe you'll find a way to be a real partner in the business."

The very thought sent a shiver through her. "I don't know that I can."

"Why not?" Lydia's voice was brisk. "You're smart, and you're a hard worker. And you don't want to turn into a fluffy pillow, ain't so?"

Halfway between laughing and crying, Beth threw a napkin at her. "All right. Don't be so bossy. I'll try. I'll go in and see what it's like, but that's all."

"Tomorrow," Lydia said firmly.

Beth wished she had another napkin to throw. "Tomorrow. I promise."

She just hoped she wouldn't regret it.

Chapter Three

For Beth, the walk down the driveway to the store the next day went too quickly. She'd agreed to spend the morning learning about the store, but that didn't mean she wanted to become part of it. Maybe she and Daniel could figure out some other way...

"Hurry up, Mammi." Benjy, in a rush as always, tugged at her hand. "I want to see what we're going to do at the store."

"I told you, remember? I must learn how the store works. And you have your jigsaw puzzle to work on and your farm animals to play with."

"Can't I help? Please?" He looked up at her, his bright blue eyes, so like his father's, pleading.

She had to guard against the temptation to give in when he looked at her that way. "You'll have plenty of time to work when you're older. Komm, let's go in."

Despite her words, she was the one who hesitated as they neared the glass door at the front of the cinder block building. She remembered the good-natured arguments between James and Daniel when they planned the store. Daniel had been cautious, thinking it should be smaller, but James had laughed at him, saying he should have more confidence in their success. In the end, James had prevailed, as he so often did.

But he'd been proved right, hadn't he? The store was a success. Grasping Benjy firmly by the hand, she pushed the door and stepped inside.

Daniel came forward immediately, smiling in welcome. "Ach, Beth, wilkom. And you, Benjy." He gestured, and the other two people in the store came forward. "You remember Anna Fisher, don't you? She's been working for us for about a year."

The teenager gave Beth a quick glance before lowering her eyes again. Given how shy Anna was, it wondered Beth that she could wait on customers, but from what James had said about her, Anna was a conscientious worker.

"It's gut to see you again, Anna. I understand the store couldn't get along without you."

A flush brightened the girl's pale cheeks. "Denke," she murmured.

Poor child. Everyone knew what a disagreeable person Hiram Fisher was, and Beth didn't imagine he was any better with his daughter. No wonder the girl looked as if she'd wilt at a sharp word.

Thinking Anna would relax once the attention was off her, Beth turned to the third person, who waited next to Daniel.

"This is one of your nephews, ain't so? Timothy, right?"

The boy grinned, his blue eyes dancing. He must be about fourteen or fifteen to be out of school, but he looked younger with that mischievous grin and the freckles that dotted his nose.

"Yah, Timothy, that's me."

"My brother Seth's oldest," Daniel added. "He's been helping us out since…for the last few weeks."

Since James died, he meant. She'd have to convince them that they didn't need to fear mentioning him, even if it was difficult.

"That's wonderful gut of you, Timothy."

"Denke." And then, as if it burst out of him, he added, "I really like it. Maybe I'll have a business of my own one day."

Daniel reached out to ruffle his hair, smiling. "You're a far distance from that just now, young Timothy. You have some stocking to do, ain't so?"

Nothing seemed to disturb Timothy's grin. "Bossy," he muttered, and drifted off. Anna took advantage of the opportunity to slip away as quietly as a mouse.

Benjy tugged at Beth's skirt. "Everybody is working, Mammi. I want to work, too."

"Not today." She handed him the bag containing his toys. "We'll find a place to set up your puzzle."

He took the bag but obviously had something else to say. "Grossdaadi said that one day part of the store would be mine. I should help."

"Not today, I said." She was aware of Daniel listening and suspected he was disapproving.

Benjy got his mulish look, but before he could say anything, Daniel intervened.

"Komm, let's find a table where you can work your puzzle." He held out his hand to Benjy. "Maybe you can help me set the table up, all right?"

One thing she could say for Benjy—he was easily distracted. He trotted along after Daniel, and she had time to breathe for a moment.

What would Daniel think of her, being so sharp with her son? She could hardly tell him why being in the place so associated with James had set her nerves on edge. Was it here that James's involvement with the woman started? It seemed likely.

But when Daniel returned after he and Benjy had set up a folding table and Benjy had dumped out the puzzle pieces, he didn't appear to be thinking any such thing.

"Since you haven't been here much, why don't we start off with a walk around, just to remind you where everything is?"

Beth nodded, and together they checked out the small break room, where the coffeepot steamed, and took a look in the storeroom, which stretched across the back of the building. Timothy was there, loading what looked like heavy boxes of canned goods onto a cart. He glanced up with a grin before turning back to the boxes.

"We have a pretty fast turnover most of the time, so we try to stay ahead of what's going to be needed," Daniel explained, gesturing toward the marked cartons. "It's been a big help having Timothy here. In fact..." He stopped, as if reconsidering what he was going to say.

Before she could ask, he'd moved on. "Here's the office. All the book work is done here. If you want to go over the books, I'll be glad to show you where everything is."

She had a quick vision of James sitting at the desk, his hair ruffled as he struggled with figures. "Not right now," she said. Then, unable to resist prodding the pain of picturing him, she added, "Did James do the record keeping?"

Daniel chuckled. "Not James. He didn't like jobs that required sitting still. He enjoyed interacting with the customers and the suppliers, so he took care of that side of things."

"It was kind of you to let him do the job he liked." But with his outgoing personality, James had probably done it well.

Daniel shrugged. "James was used to getting his way."

She gave him a sharp look, but it was apparent that wasn't meant as an insult. It was simply the truth. James did usually get his way, and things seemed to turn out as he wanted.

When they got back to the store proper, several customers had come in. Anna was busy in the baked goods section, leaving no one at the checkout counter. Beth expected Daniel to head there, but instead he gave her a hopeful look.

"Would you mind running the checkout counter for a bit? A fresh produce order should be coming in, and I need to talk with the driver. There's an adding machine on the counter, and the price should be marked on everything."

"I guess I could do that." She felt shy taking it on,

but surely it couldn't be that hard. If she kept busy, maybe she'd stop picturing James everywhere she turned.

The gratitude in Daniel's face chided her. She had given little thought, enmeshed in her own misery, for how this affected Daniel and the business.

"I'll shout if I need help, yah?"

Daniel's smile lit his normally serious face, making her think of how James had teased him, saying it made him look like an old man. Pushing the thought away, she hurried to the counter.

The first couple of checkouts were easy. The customers were from her own church district, so all of them had already had opportunities to express their condolences. They still all commented on how good it was to see her out of the house, but she could handle that.

Several people commented on the Honeycrisp apples, knowing that they'd have come from her orchard. She was a little surprised at the lift that gave her. The fruits of the orchard were her products, maybe that was why.

By taking a few steps, she could see around the nearest counter to where Benjy sat. He'd been working on his puzzle, but soon he had given that up, and he seemed to be putting his miniature farm animals into and out of a barn improvised from a box.

When she turned back to the counter, she recognized Ellen Schultz heading toward her, wearing an expression composed of sorrow and curiosity mixed. Beth braced herself. Ellen belonged to the sister church district, which shared the same bishop, so this was her opportunity to express condolences.

"Ach, Beth, I didn't think to see you in the store. Poor thing." Ellen grasped her hand, and ready tears welled in the woman's eyes. "I'm that sorry for your loss. James is safe with God, but you are left to carry on, ain't so?"

Clearly the woman didn't expect an answer. That was just as well, since Beth didn't have one. Would James be with the Lord, despite the pain and betrayal he'd left behind? She hadn't considered it, and she didn't want to.

"Denke, Ellen. You're so kind."

As she added up Ellen's bill and collected the money, she let the flow of commiserations go in one ear and out the other. How long, she wondered, would it take for people to stop thinking of her as "poor Beth"?

With a few more expressions of sympathy, Ellen carried her packages out the door. Beth took a deep breath, relieved that no one else was headed to the counter at the moment. She'd just check on Benjy...

She moved the few steps that let her see the table. The table was there all right, with Benjy's puzzle scattered on top of it and the farm animals in their barn. But Benjy wasn't there. Panic gripped her heart. Benjy was gone.

Daniel was carrying a carton of lettuce through the storeroom when Beth rushed through the door, her face white and her eyes filled with panic. Shoving the carton onto the nearest table, he raced toward her.

"Beth, what's wrong? What happened?"

"Benjy! I can't find Benjy." She stared frantically around the storeroom. "Benjy! Are you in here?"

"Easy, slow down." He clasped her arm to keep her from rushing off. "He can't have gone far. Are you sure he isn't in the store?"

"He's gone. I just turned away for a few minutes to check out a customer, and when I looked again, he wasn't there." Her voice shook on the words.

"He probably got bored and went to look around, that's all. Komm, you can't help by panicking. I'll help you look."

Beth shot him an angry glance, but then she sucked in a breath and nodded.

They separated to move quickly through the storeroom, although Daniel felt reasonably sure the boy couldn't have gotten in. The latch on the storeroom door was too high for Benjy to reach, he'd think.

They met back at the door. "He must be in the store," he said, trying to keep any doubt out of his voice. For sure Benjy would be there. Where else could he be?

"Just stay calm," he said, holding the door for her. "There's nowhere else he could have gone."

Her eyes widened, as if what he'd said had frightened her. "The door. What if he slipped outside? It's so close to the road—" She didn't finish, just darted toward the front door.

Daniel let her go, knowing there was no sense in trying to stop her. She was frightened, and that wasn't surprising. Only a month ago she'd buried her husband, and the responsibility for their child must weigh heavily on her. The best thing he could do was to look for Benjy himself in the most likely places. He started through the aisles.

And sure enough, the most likely place it was. Benjy stood behind a stack of boxes, peering around them at Timothy, who was unloading cans of vegetables.

Safe enough. And natural, too, that the boy would be looking for some activity after sitting so long. Any smart, active four-year-old would want to be part of things.

Leaving them without speaking, Daniel headed for the front door. Through the glass door he could see Beth looking up and down the road for any glimpse of her son. The anguish on her face ripped at his heart.

He covered the remaining space to the door in a few swift strides, shoved it open and reached her. "It's all right. He's fine. He's inside."

Beth's green eyes, dark with worry, searched his face and saw the confidence there. She let out a long breath. "Thank the gut Lord. Where is he?" She started toward the door, as if to rush in and scoop him up.

He clasped her wrist to stop her, feeling it pound against his palm. "Wait, Beth. Calm down. Benjy doesn't think he's missing. You don't want to scare him, ain't so?"

For an instant he thought she'd flare up at him, but then she seemed to struggle for control. She took a deep breath, and then another.

"You're right. I guess I overreacted. When he wasn't where I expected him to be, it just seemed to wash me off my feet."

"I know. With everything…with losing James…it's natural you'd be off balance."

She nodded. Letting out another long breath, she managed a slight smile. "All right. I can behave now. Let's go in."

They walked back toward the canned goods, and he could almost feel the tension in her making her long to grab Benjy and fuss over him. He was tempted to repeat his warning, but if she resented it, he'd have done more harm than good.

When they reached the last row of shelves, Beth stood quietly, just watching the two boys. Relieved, he stood behind her and looked over her shoulder.

Benjy stood next to Timothy, who was kneeling on the floor, transferring cans from the boxes to the shelves. "…each kind of vegetable has its own place," Timothy was explaining. "See, I look at the picture on the can and then at the cans on the shelf. This one is corn, so where do you think it goes?"

His small face serious, Benjy studied the shelves. "There!" he said, triumph in his voice. He pointed to the right place, and Timothy, grinning, put the can in its spot.

"Gut." Benjy hesitated. "Can I put some on the shelves? I could help you."

Now it was Timothy's turn to hesitate. "If your mammi says it's okay." He nodded toward them. "Why don't you ask her?"

Benjy spun around, seeing them for the first time. "Can I, Mammi? Can I help Timothy?"

The last of Beth's tension seemed gone. "If Timothy

is willing to show you, that's fine. But mind, if he has to do something else, you don't pester him. All right?"

Benjy's smile was like sunshine breaking through the clouds. "I won't, Mammi. I'll do just what Timothy says."

"Gut." Beth turned, coming face-to-face with Daniel. He stepped back. He was pleased to see her smiling as they walked away.

"I hadn't thought of that," she murmured. "That's how we learned, yah? By standing next to someone, learning and then trying it ourselves."

"That's it, for sure. Remember when your onkel taught us how to pick the apples? He was a patient man, letting a bunch of kids like us loose in his orchard."

"I remember." Her face eased into a smile. "Denke, Daniel. I'm glad I brought Benjy."

By the next afternoon, Beth regretted she'd said those words. Benjy seemed determined to turn their visit to the store into a regular routine. He was dismayed to find they weren't heading out first thing the following morning. After his third complaint, Beth knelt beside him.

"I know you like going to the store, and we'll do it again. But not today," she added, before he could burst into speech. "This afternoon the cousins are coming to pick apples again, remember? We have to be here."

Benjy wasn't one to be discouraged at a single obstacle. "But this morning—"

"This morning I have my regular work to do so I

can be free for the apple-picking. And you're going to clean up your bedroom."

The firmness in her voice must have told him argument was useless. He headed toward the stairs, his steps dragging. Suppressing a smile, she turned back to the breakfast dishes.

Benjy was a good boy. He liked to get his own way, but what four-year-old didn't? If he had a little brother or sister, he'd have learned to be more flexible, she supposed. Now...well, now she couldn't see that it would ever happen. She'd have to take extra care not to spoil him.

Despite Benjy's enthusiasm for the store, she couldn't help wondering how long it would last if she committed to working a regular schedule. She could have someone watch him, but she hated the idea of leaving her little one with someone else.

But how else could she do her share of the work? The business belonged to her and Daniel now, and it wasn't fair to him if she didn't contribute something to the store. The issue swirled around and around in her mind, making her dizzy with indecision. She felt a wave of anger toward James for dying and leaving her in this predicament, and an instant later she fell to her knees, praying for forgiveness.

"Mammi?" Benjy's voice penetrated her misery. "What's wrong? Did you fall down?"

The tremor in his voice brought her back to her senses. She pressed her palms against the braided rug in front of the sink.

"No, no, I'm fine. I thought I dropped a pin, that's

all." She rose. "All finished upstairs?" At his nod, she went on. "Let's go out and check for eggs, then."

Benjy was easily distracted, but her conscience continued to trouble her for the next few hours. Anger might be a natural response, but for the faithful, it was one to be conquered. Whatever wrong James had done, it was vanished in God's forgiveness now.

Beth had just cleared up from lunch when she heard the rattle of the wagon coming down the drive.

"Mammi, they're here!" Benjy had been perched on the back porch steps, watching eagerly for any sign of his cousins.

"I'm coming." She hurried out to welcome them, surprised to see Daniel sitting in the back of the wagon next to her brother Eli and several of her nieces and nephews.

"Wilkom. I can see we'll get a lot of picking done this afternoon with all this help."

"Hop on," Daad said. "We'll take the wagon up to the orchard so we can load easily."

"You go ahead. I'll fetch the baskets."

Even as she was speaking, Daniel slid down and lifted Benjy into the wagon. "I'll give you a hand," he said.

"Denke, but shouldn't you be at the store this afternoon?"

"I thought it would be gut for Anna to be left in charge for a bit. Besides, the sooner we get the apples picked, the faster we'll sell them. I've had folks asking for them."

Giving in, she led the way to the shed where she'd

stored the baskets. He bent to pick up a stack of them, and she followed suit, wondering if he were trying to make her feel good about the apples. But it was true that the first few baskets they'd taken in had sold quickly.

Beth half expected him to bring up the idea of her coming to work at the store on a regular basis, but he didn't, just chatting easily about the orchard and reminding her of other days of apple-picking.

When they reached the early apple trees, Daniel dropped his stack of baskets and began to hand them out.

Daad grabbed one. "Let's get started. Eli, you and Daniel might bring the stepladder. I don't want these young ones climbing too high."

"Ach, we can do it, Grossdaadi." Eli's twelve-year-old, Joshua, was brimming with confidence, and she hoped Benjy wasn't going to emulate him.

"The last time you climbed too high and Daadi had to get the ladder to bring you down," Janie said, flattening him as only an older sister could.

"That was years ago," he protested.

Eli and Daniel, coming from the shed with the stepladder, overheard some of it, and Eli frowned at both of them. "No fussing, you two. And, Joshua, you listen to Aunt Beth. They are her trees, ain't so?"

Joshua grinned, unrepentant. "Yah, I will."

"That one's as full of mischief as his daadi was," Daniel commented, seizing a basket. "I remember Eli clowning around when we were picking once and breaking a branch. Your onkel laid into him something fierce."

Before Beth could answer, Benjy tugged at her skirt. "Mammi, where's my basket? I have to pick."

"Right here," Daniel said quickly. "You and I are partners, ain't so?"

"Yah!" Benjy's face lit up, and he grabbed the basket. "Hurry, before they pick all the apples."

"We can't let that happen." His eyes laughing, Daniel winked at Beth and went off with her son.

Beth stood where she was for a moment, not sure how she felt about letting Benjy go off with someone else. *Foolish*, she scolded herself. *You can trust Daniel, and you don't want to tie Benjy to your apron strings.*

Grabbing a basket, she headed for the tree where young Janie was picking.

"The apples are wonderful gut," Janie said, putting her foot in the crotch of the tree and moving higher. She'd hung a smaller basket around her waist so that she didn't have to climb up and down and was picking with quick, deft motions.

"Yah, they are. It's the best crop of Honeycrisp we've had in several years. They're choosy about the weather." She seemed to hear her uncle's voice echoing in her head. "That's what Onkel Isaac always said."

Janie nodded. "You'll be able to sell a lot in the store." She hesitated, looking as if she wanted to say something more.

Beth smiled at her, thinking how dear this sweet niece was to her. "Did you want to ask me something, Janie?"

Smiling back, she ducked her head. "I was just thinking... Daadi said you maybe would be working in the store more. If you are, I could watch Benjy for you, couldn't I?"

Every member of her family seemed to think they knew what she ought to do. Or what she planned to, which was more than she did. Still, this was the obvious answer to one of her concerns.

"I don't know yet what I'm going to do," she said carefully. "But if I do work at the store, I think that would be a fine idea."

Janie's eyes danced, probably at the idea of having an actual job. "I'd like that. Anytime you need me."

Putting a couple of apples in her basket, Beth stretched her back. When she looked across the orchard, she could see Daniel holding Benjy up to pick some apples high over his head.

Benjy showed no fear, she realized. He trusted Daniel just as he trusted his family. He wasn't afraid of the future.

The thought struck her. Was that what was behind her reluctance to take her place as Daniel's partner? Fear?

There was no need for fear. Wariness, maybe. She didn't think she could ever trust a man in the way she'd trusted James—blindly sure that she knew him. But it wasn't that holding her paralyzed.

She felt as if she were poised on a stone in a rushing creek, longing to stay in the familiar place, but knowing she couldn't. Knowing it had already crumbled under her feet.

It was time to move forward. Everyone, it seemed, knew that but her.

Beth set her basket down. "I'll be back in a minute, Janie."

Without waiting for a response, she headed toward Daniel. When he spotted her, he lowered Benjy to the ground, watching her warily.

Did he think she was going to protest his boosting Benjy up in the tree?

"Are you two getting lots of apples?"

Benjy beamed at the question. "Look, Mammi. Me and Daniel picked half a basket already."

Beth touched his soft cheek. "We always put the other person first, remember?"

He ducked his head. "Daniel and me."

Daniel's mouth twitched at that, and she had to suppress a smile. At the moment she was teaching the Amish way, not grammar.

"Better," she said. She looked up at Daniel. "I just wanted to ask. Which is best for the business—for me to work mornings or afternoons?"

He understood, and his face lit much as Benjy's had. "Either is gut. Denke, Beth. I'm glad."

She took a deep breath and tried to settle the qualms she felt. She'd committed herself now, and she'd have to go through with it.

Chapter Four

Beth held Benjy's hand as they walked out the driveway early the next morning. She tried not to smile at his solemn expression as he trotted along beside her, very conscious of his black suit and white shirt. The serious nature of his Sunday clothing always made him just a little more eager to appear grown up, not that any clothing could do that. The sweet curve of his neck and his rosy cheeks still reminded her of babyhood.

She couldn't say that she took much pleasure from her widow's black clothing. Not that she was prideful about her appearance—that would be wrong. But black seemed to draw all the color from her face, making her look older than her years. Or maybe it was the grief and pain that had this effect.

They reached the road and fell in with the other families from along their road. Worship this morning was at Sam and Miriam Shuler's barn, no more than a half mile away. Had it been much farther she'd have waited for Mamm and Daad to pick her up in the family carriage. They had offered to stop for her today, but she relished the quiet walk. It gave time for reflection, something generally missing from her busy life.

The fields on either side of the road had begun to show a glimpse of gold as the weather cooled down. This morning was a bit brisk, but the sun promised a warm afternoon.

"Today is the first Sunday of preparing for fall Communion." She spoke softly to Benjy, wondering whether to warn him that the service might go longer than usual. "We all want to prepare our hearts for Communion."

He considered that for a moment. Did he remember the conversation they'd had prior to spring Communion? Whether he did or not, it was good to reinforce the teaching. The burden of her son's training in Amish ways was solely hers now.

"What should I do?" he said finally.

"We settle our hearts on the Lord, and we forgive anyone against whom we have been angry." She had more to say, but the words dried up on her tongue.

Anger and forgiveness. She had been angry, and try as she might to lose that anger, it flared up again and again. Her heart cramped. If she had not reached forgiveness of James and of the woman who had ruined her happiness, she wouldn't be able to take Communion. What would that say to her son, as well as the rest of the community?

Please, Lord. She tried to find the words to forgive, but each time she tried, her heart rebelled. *Please, Lord, show me how to forgive. Please.*

Grossmammi had reminded her to talk to God, that He would be listening. But right now she felt as if she prayed into emptiness.

They'd reached the farm road, and it was a short walk to the barn. Those who had already arrived were gathering outside. Benjy spotted his grandparents, tugged his hand free and hurried to them, trying not to run.

By the time Beth reached her parents and grandmother, Benjy was talking a mile a minute to his grandfather. She could only be glad he was doing it in a soft voice.

Her grandmother smiled at her expression. "He's trying," she murmured. "Best to let him get it out before he goes in to worship."

"I know. Three hours is a long time for such a chatterbox to keep quiet."

"Ach, let him be," her mother said indulgently. "I love to hear him talk. He's so bright and happy it gives us joy to hear him."

"You can be the one to keep him quiet during the service, then," she teased. "He's certain sure not like me when I was his age."

Unfortunately, the words just reminded her that Benjy took after his father in that respect. She said a panicked prayer that that was the only way he resembled James.

She had to stop thinking this way. It would soon be time to go into the barn. It might be only a barn, but when the community was gathered together, the Lord was there. She couldn't carry angry thoughts with her.

The business of finding her place in the line of young married woman distracted her attention. There were welcoming smiles, and more than one person clasped her hand briefly in passing. She exchanged smiles with Lydia, still in the group of unmarried women. Her gaze was caught by Daniel, who gave her the solemn nod that was appropriate to worship, and then her line passed into the barn.

Settling Benjy next to her on the backless bench, she considered getting something out of the small bag of toys and snacks she'd brought, but at the moment he was looking around happily, so she left it.

There, in the silence, she prepared her heart for worship, knowing already that today's service would be focused on Nicodemus and new life in Christ. The worship year followed its traditional pattern. In two weeks it would be Council Meeting Sunday, with its emphasis on giving and receiving forgiveness. And the worship after that would be Communion. It wasn't much time, it seemed, to find her way to forgiveness.

The lead singer sounded the first wavering note of a hymn, and worship had begun.

When the final hymn had been sung and the final prayer said, the quiet atmosphere of worship gave way to the bustle of preparing for lunch. Several women—the hostess, her daughters, her sisters and close friends—hurried toward the kitchen to begin carrying food out. Meanwhile the men and older boys started transforming the benches into the tables that would be used for their meal together.

"Mammi, can I go find my cousins?" Benjy wiggled with pleasure at no longer being still.

"Put your toys back in the bag first, and then you may." She held it open while he hurriedly dropped his small horse and buggy in place.

He scurried off and she followed more slowly, intent on finding Lydia. Lydia seemed to have the same thought in mind, because she was there in a moment, putting her arm around Beth's waist as if they were ten again.

"All right?" she asked, keeping her voice low. "I thought the first Sunday after…" She let that trail off, glancing around.

"Yah. It was difficult, but I'm fine."

Lydia's scrutiny said she doubted it. The barn was emptying out, and they walked slowly toward the door together.

"The thing is…" It would be a relief to unburden herself to Lydia, but she was ashamed of some of the thoughts she'd had during worship.

"What?" Lydia pinched her. "Komm on, I know there's something. Spill it. I'm hungry."

That made her smile, as Lydia had known it would. "Are you ten or twenty-four? Hungry sounds like Benjy. He's probably pestering his grossmammi for a snack right now."

"I intend to pester you until I get an answer, and I can pester a lot better than Benjy. Tell me. Have you found out something?"

Her nerves jumped at the thought. "No, not really. But when I looked over at you during the second sermon, I realized I was seeing all the unmarried women of the community sitting on the same bench. It made me wonder…" She stumbled to a halt.

"You wonder if it was one of them." Lydia's blue eyes grew somber. "Yah, I have to say I've been thinking that, too. But it doesn't have to be, you know. It could just as easily be someone from a nearby community. Or a married woman. Or even an Englischer. Working in the store, he had to meet plenty of them."

"I've thought of that. It's getting so every woman I look at makes me wonder. *Was it you? Are you the one who stole James from me?*"

Lydia's eyes flashed. "James had something to do with it, too, ain't so?"

"I know, I know. I'm not saying he didn't. But the thing is, I know I have to forgive them if I'm ever going to stop going around in circles. And how can I forgive her when I don't know who it was?"

Lydia looked troubled. "Ach, Beth, surely it is best not to know. Not to picture the two of them together."

"I still picture them," Beth blurted out. "I just can't see her face."

Lydia gave her a quick hug. "Let it go, Beth. It's a terrible bad thing, but you have to get past it."

Not even Lydia understood, it seemed. She spoke with sudden clarity. "I can't do that. I have to know. I have to know who the woman was. I have to."

Leaning against the fence, Daniel joined in the talk after worship about Sam's new pair of draft horses—

Percherons, they were, and a fine-looking pair with strongly muscled bodies.

"Sam says he got a gut deal on the pair of them. He went clear down to Lancaster County for them." Daniel's older brother Seth, who was taking over the dairy farm from Daad, stood beside him. As if they knew they were being admired, the massive animals raised their heads to gaze back at them.

"Sam's got his heart's desire, I guess," Daad said, eyes twinkling. "Everyone knows he's been trying to convince Miriam for a couple of years now."

The group of men chuckled, and someone moved the talk on to the price soybeans were bringing and the possibility of planting a few more acres in the spring.

Daniel could almost list the topics of conversation from memory. Every other Sunday the men gathered after worship to exchange talk of farming, lumber, dairying and the work of the coming month. He'd guess that the women were doing the same thing, only their subjects would be babies, fabric, the best place to buy children's shoes and who would host the next quilting bee.

Those frequent conversations seemed to make up the patchwork of Amish life, creating the dense, tight fabric that meant being Amish. His gaze roamed the farmyard—the children playing, the teenage girls watching the babies, the women either carrying food or clustered in small groups, heads together.

He glimpsed Beth in a clutch of young married women, the people she had the most in common with, he supposed. But even as he watched, she slipped out of the group, her black dress contrasting with the blues and dark greens the other women wore.

Did she feel uncomfortable with them now that she was a widow? Maybe so, because she went quickly to her mother and grandmother, maybe taking refuge in the family circle.

He pulled his attention back to the group, and just in time, because Elijah Schmidt mentioned his name.

"...hear tell that Beth Esch is working at the store now. That right?"

Something in him resented the question—in fact, any mention of her by someone who was fairly new to the district and couldn't claim to have known her since childhood.

"Yah," he said, hoping the short answer would deter the man.

Elijah didn't seem to get the message. He shook his head, frowning. "Hope she's not thinking she can take her husband's place in the partnership. That sort of work would never do for a young woman like her."

Annoyance rumbled inside him, but before he could speak, his daad chipped in. "It's not like Daniel will have her unloading trucks. That's what young Timothy is there for."

Seth grinned. "If Daniel can get a day's work out of the boy, that's enough to make me happy. He'll never make a farmer, that's certain sure."

"You have other sons," Daad said. "It's never wise to set a youngster's hand to the wrong plow."

Several other fathers nodded in agreement. Usually in every Amish family there'd be one destined to be a farmer. Seth's second boy showed every sign of being the one, even though he was just ten. At least they'd gotten Elijah off the subject of Beth.

But it seemed Daniel was wrong, because Elijah brought it up again almost immediately. "Now, what the widow ought to do is sell her share in the business. I wouldn't mind owning half a thriving business like that myself. What do you suppose it's worth?"

Daniel couldn't control himself any longer, but before he could find the words to say what he thought, Seth broke in, his face suddenly solemn. His deacon's face, the children called it.

"The Sabbath is not the time, and this isn't the place for talking business." His tone was so severe Daniel almost didn't recognize it.

In any event, it seemed to abash Elijah. Muttering something that might have been an apology, he turned away just as the lunch bell rang. Everyone started moving to where the long tables were ready with the usual after-worship lunch.

Daniel fell into step with his brother and father. "Denke," he murmured. "It seems it takes a deacon's word to shut Elijah's mouth."

Seth grinned and nudged him. "Thought I'd best intervene before you said something you might regret. It's fortunate for him that he didn't say that around one of Beth's brothers or he'd have gotten the wrong side of the tongue for his trouble."

"Yah." Daniel figured it best to agree, although he didn't think he'd regret anything he might have said to the man. "You have to extend wilkom to a newcomer, but Elijah doesn't seem to fit in very well. I just hope he doesn't say anything to Beth. It would upset her."

Seth nodded his agreement. "How is Beth getting along? Mary Ann says she's going to take a meal over sometime this week and ask if there's anything we can do to help with the orchard."

"It's early yet, but she seems to want to do her share with the store. She's planning to work a few hours each day to start."

Daad frowned a bit, his thick, graying eyebrows seeming to bristle. "You'd best make sure she doesn't do too much. It takes time to heal from a loss like hers."

"I know. I'll keep an eye on her." He saw the white, strained expression Beth sometimes wore. "Seems to me it's doing her gut to get out of the house and talk to people."

"You'll know, I expect. You two were always close when you were small. In fact, your mamm and I thought that the two of you would make a match of it."

The only safe thing Daniel could do was nod, but Daad's casual comment sent his thoughts spiraling back to his teens—to the evening at a singing when he'd quite suddenly stopped thinking of Beth as a tomboy friend and seen her as a young woman. And known he loved her.

Strange, that it was that same evening when James began looking at Beth in a new way, too. James, who charmed every girl, hadn't yet tried his charm on Beth, but he was abruptly sure she was the girl he wanted. Beth, like every other girl, fell victim to his easy, laughing smile.

He'd stepped away. What else could he do, when James was his best friend? God was wise in not letting anyone know the future. James had brought Beth to grief in the end. Still, she'd never had to learn anything negative about him while he was still with her.

Did that make it any better? He wasn't sure.

By Tuesday morning, Beth was beginning to get used to her new routine, and Benjy had fallen into it as if it were normal. They arrived before the store opened, and once she had Benjy settled with something to do, she helped set up for the day.

Benjy seemed happy enough to play in a corner Daniel had set up for him with room for a few toys, books and games, so she hadn't yet called on her niece to babysit. She should do that soon, so that Benjy could spend more time outdoors while the nice weather lasted. Janie would jump at the chance, she knew.

She started toward the checkout counter and then paused, noticing Anna doing the same. Anna was still so shy and reserved around her, and she didn't want to make the girl think she was taking over her job.

Daniel appeared next to her, so she didn't have to make a decision. "I asked Anna to take the checkout first this morning so we could spend some time on how the storeroom is arranged and stocked, if that's okay with you."

"For sure. I thought we should be venturing into there soon. Just let me tell Benjy where I'll be." She detoured around the end of a counter to where Benjy was creating what was probably a barn from some blocks.

"I'm going in the storeroom to work for a little while."

"Can I come, too?" he asked, before she could even finish what she was going to say.

"Not this time. I'll show you what I've learned later. If you need any help, Anna is at the counter. You can ask her, yah?" She'd noticed that Anna wasn't nearly as shy with Benjy as she was with adults.

He pouted a little but then went back to his blocks without a word. She would talk to Janie later today, she resolved. Benjy would be better for a break.

"Okay?" Daniel raised his eyebrows as they walked to the back of the store.

She nodded. "Daniel, I was wondering…does Anna think I'm taking over her job?"

"No, not that I know of, but maybe I haven't been noticing. Has she said something to make you think so?"

"She hasn't said anything at all…well, very little. I know she's rather shy, and I haven't wanted to push her. But I'm not that scary, am I?"

He chuckled. "Not that I've ever noticed. Except for the time one of my brothers put your doll up in the apple tree. You were plenty scary over that, as I remember."

She couldn't help smiling. "I was plenty mad. And I never knew for sure who it was. Are you trying to convince me it wasn't you?"

"I shouldn't have said that—the boys all had a pact not to give each other away." He pushed open the door to the storeroom.

Still smiling, Beth walked in. Talking about those happy times was like taking a little rest from today's worries and griefs.

"Anyway, about Anna..." Daniel took a clipboard from a nail on the wall as he spoke. "I'd guess she's not sure how to talk to someone who has so recently lost a spouse." He gave her a sidelong glance, as if to be sure he wasn't causing her pain by mentioning it.

"Please." She reached out impulsively to Daniel. "Please just talk normally about James. The worst thing is to have people trying to avoid saying his name." No matter what she knew about him, James had been her husband and the father of her son. Grief was expected and normal.

As for the thing that wasn't normal—well, she had to find her own way of dealing with it.

Seeming reassured, Daniel gestured to the clipboards on the wall. "This is the main thing I wanted to show you. Each company or person who delivers merchandise has a sheet of their own. It's easier to keep track of that way. This one is for Larks Suppliers. They provide crackers, cookies, packaged chips...that kind of thing, and they usually come about twice a month. When you check them in—"

"Me?"

She glanced up in time to see a slightly guilty look on his face. "Sorry. I guess I should have mentioned that first. I have to make a trip out to the lumberyard to pick up some supplies. Do you mind doing the check-in if Larks comes before I get back?"

Beth pushed down a moment of doubt. Of course,

she could do this. It was part of running the store, after all.

"No, I don't mind. As long as you don't mind if I make a mistake."

"I'm not afraid of that happening." His tone was light, his eyes amused.

Daniel's face didn't give much away, but when you knew him, you realized that his eyes told you everything you needed to know. If she had to have a partner, she was fortunate that it was an old friend like Daniel.

Chapter Five

Daniel went off to the lumberyard, and they were on their own. Beth felt confident of her abilities right up to the moment when she heard the buzzer that announced someone at the loading dock. Then her pulse jumped, and her voice went dry.

Silly, she told herself, and marched back to the storeroom. She paused, momentarily forgetting how the loading dock worked, but then she spotted the pulley running along the right side. The pulley system made it easy to open the large doors at the dock, and once she'd done that successfully, her confidence began to return.

The Englisch driver gave her a cheerful wave and, as he drew closer, a curious look. He probably realized she was someone new.

"Good day. Just let me get the clipboard, and I'll check in the order." She tried to sound as if she did it every day, but suspected she'd failed.

"Right you are." He swung himself up to the back of the truck like a young man, although he had to be in his forties at least, with thinning hair partially hidden by a ball cap and the beginnings of a paunch. His brightly colored T-shirt stretched across it.

Hurrying back to the opposite wall, she seized the Larks clipboard, quickly scanning the form. Simple enough, she thought. All she had to do was list the items delivered and the number of them.

The driver was already unloading, so she hurried to find the contents on the outside of the cartons. Filling in the name was easy, since she was familiar with most of the products. The amount baffled her until she realized it was the number of cartons, not the individual bags.

The driver's curiosity got the better of him as he stacked cartons of crackers. "You're new here, right?"

Beth nodded. "I started last week." There was no reason to get into details with the man. "You have a nice day for your deliveries." The sun had burned off the early morning fog that was so typical in the fall.

"Sure is. Let's see now." He stood back, checking his own list to compare it with what he'd brought. "Sure you don't want another case of those sea salt chips? They're selling fast."

"Just what's on the list." Beth softened the refusal with a smile. She certainly wouldn't venture to order something on her own, not yet.

He shrugged, holding out a receipt for her signature. "Nice seeing you. You're a lot prettier than the guy who usually helped me. James, his name is. He off today?"

Her stomach cramped. She should have realized the drivers would be familiar with James. And she certain sure shouldn't have let herself be jolted just by his name.

"He's not with us anymore." There, that was all she need say.

The driver nodded, swinging himself up to his seat. He leaned out for a final word. "Not surprised he got the ax. Probably chased out of town by a jealous husband, right?"

He slammed his door and drove off, leaving her standing frozen.

How long she'd have stood there completely numb, she didn't know. She was shaken into movement by the sound of footsteps behind her. Trying to hold herself together, she turned, not quite looking at Timothy.

"I'll get that." He reached past her to close the door. "That was Tom Ellis, yah? Did he talk your ear off?"

"N-not quite." She gestured toward the boxes, shielding her expression with the clipboard. "These are all checked in. Do you know what to do with them now?"

"Yah, sure. I'll do that as long as you take care of the paperwork. Onkel Daniel doesn't trust me with that since I marked down a dozen packages instead of a dozen cases."

He didn't seem very upset, lifting several boxes in his arms. He looked at her quickly, and then his gaze moved away just as fast. "Everything okay?"

Beth pulled herself together. "Yah, sure. I'll just go…" She let that trail off. What she wanted to do was to be alone someplace where she could cry and yell if she wanted to. She couldn't do that, but maybe she could find some privacy.

Walking quickly back into the store, she paused. She wanted to hurry into the office and shut the door, but she'd better check on Benjy and see if Anna needed her first.

Before she reached them, Anna raised her hand to catch Beth's attention. She hurried to the counter, where Anna was loading baked goods into a bag for a young and pretty Englisch woman.

"Will you… Would you mind taking my place for a few minutes?" She raised her eyes long enough to indicate the restroom.

"Yah, of course." What else could she say? She slid behind the counter and put the last few items into the woman's bag. She had the usual things the Englisch looked for when they came here—the fresh fruit and vegetables along with the baked pastries and homemade soups.

"There you are." She forced herself to smile at the woman. What she wanted to do was to ask the questions that pounded in her mind. *Did my husband flirt with you? Did he arrange to meet you somewhere?*

Before she could do something so foolish, Benjy came trotting around the corner. "Timothy says I can help him put out the crackers and cookies. Can I, Mammi?"

His smile sent enough warmth through her to slightly thaw her frozen heart. "Yah, but you must do what Timothy tells you."

"I will." He was turning already to race back to Timothy.

Another customer moved to the counter—the sort of person who fussed about everything. Were the squash really fresh? Didn't she have any better spinach? Why didn't they have any bananas?

It took all the patience she could find to deal with her when what she wanted was to throw something. She stepped back with relief when Anna returned.

"Denke, Anna." She spun and hurried to the office before anyone could stop her.

Safely inside, she closed the door and leaned back against it. She could hardly lock it without raising the questions she wanted to avoid, but at least she was alone for the moment.

Burying her face in her hands, Beth stumbled toward the desk. Now that she could cry, the need for tears had left her. She stared, dry-eyed, at the calendar on the far wall, trying to think.

She should not have been so shocked by the driver's comment. Wasn't it what she'd been thinking herself...that James hadn't saved his charm for her? He'd been exercising it on other women so openly that even strangers noticed it.

If strangers saw it enough to make jokes about it, what were the Leit saying? Her heart sank. The members of her own church family must have been talking about it.

A rational thought stopped her before she could go too far down that road. It could not have been so obvious, could it? If so, the ministers or the bishop would have spoken to James. At least, no matter how humiliating it was, it hadn't reached that level.

Anger surged through her again. Was that all she

had left to be thankful for? That James hadn't exposed them to the church's discipline with his behavior?

The door behind her rattled. She spun around and then wished she hadn't. Daniel stood there, and his expression made it clear he saw that something was wrong.

Daniel was aghast at the look on Beth's face. What on earth could have happened in the short time he'd been gone? Two quick strides took him to her.

"Ach, Beth. Don't look that way. Whatever happened, it will be all right."

He shouldn't have asked her to take care of the delivery. It was too soon to expect her to jump right into the running of the store. What was wrong with him?

She shook her head, her eyes brimming with tears she obviously tried to hold back.

"It doesn't matter if there's a problem with the delivery. We'll straighten it out in no time."

He was trying to comfort her, but the anger in her face told him he was on the wrong track.

"Delivery! Do you think I'm so stupid I can't do something so simple?" She raised the clipboard, shoving it at him. "There, you see?"

"Yah, of course you can." Whatever he said was wrong, clearly. But what had happened to get her into such a state in a short time?

But that quickly the brief flash of spirit was gone, replaced by a pain he could almost feel. "Please, tell me."

Beth looked away from him, biting her lip. "He... the driver..."

"Tom Ellis? What did he do to upset you?" It was hard to imagine Tom getting out of line with her.

"He asked where James was. I just said he wasn't here any longer. And then he said—" She stopped, swallowing hard. "He said somebody's husband must have chased him out of town."

So that was it. Had Beth really been so oblivious to James's flirting? Apparently so. Now he had to smooth this over as best he could.

"Ach, Beth, you can't get upset at anything Tom says. He didn't realize James had passed away, and he always has to tease. He didn't mean anything."

Her head came up, eyes flashing. "I'm not a baby, Daniel. Don't treat me like one. The man meant something by saying that, and I want to know what it was."

Daniel's mind swung wildly through the possibilities. He couldn't lie to her, but he couldn't bear to hurt her more than she was already hurting.

There was nothing for it but the truth, spoken as gently as possible.

"Maybe Tom had the wrong impression of James. After all, he only saw him for a few minutes each time he came by. You know what James was like. With such a lively personality, he couldn't help but chat with every customer. They enjoyed it."

"I guess they did," she said, her voice somber and a little husky from holding back tears. "We both know James was a charmer, ain't so? Was he flirting with some of the Englisch customers?"

He had to answer when she looked at him that way,

as if trusting him for the truth. "You could call it that, but he wouldn't do anything out of line. You know that."

"Do I?" She seemed to wilt. "I'm not sure what I know anymore. And you… Would you be trying to cover up for your oldest friend?"

"Beth…" He took her hands in his, unable to suppress the need to comfort her. "James wasn't my oldest friend. You are. No matter that we were friends and partners, I wouldn't lie to you for him."

He wasn't lying. His suspicion wasn't a fact, and he couldn't speak of it to her.

She was very close, and when she looked up at him, he could see the darkness in the green eyes that were usually as clear as glass. If he'd given her more pain…

She put her hands up to her face, and he knew she was crying silently. His heart twisted. He put his arm around her, patting her shoulder.

Daniel's conscience pricked him. He didn't just want to comfort Beth. He wanted…

No. He couldn't let himself feel this way for his friend's wife. But he couldn't seem to control it, and he couldn't push her away when she needed comfort so badly.

Beth must have been hit by the same thought. He could feel it in the way she stiffened. She took a step away from him. She wiped her eyes with her fingers, hiding her face from him.

"Beth…" He struggled to find words.

"I'm sorry. I didn't mean to…to make you uncomfortable. I'm sorry," she said again.

"It's nothing." He tried to sound normal. "Everybody needs to let their feelings out sometime. We'll forget it, yah?"

She forced a smile through the tears. "Yah. Denke." She hurried away, heading back to the restroom to repair the trace of tears, he supposed.

And he was left wondering what he should do. If he spoke of his suspicions to Beth, it wasn't only a question of betraying his friend. He would hurt Beth even more than she'd already been hurt.

But if he kept quiet, and then she found out… There were no good answers.

Beth found she was still brooding on the incident when she was doing the dishes after supper. It was foolish to dwell on such a small thing as leaning on a friend, but all the determination in the world couldn't seem to wipe it from her mind.

She had needed comfort in the wake of what she'd heard from the driver. She'd have turned to anyone who happened to offer sympathy, to Lydia or Grossmammi, but of course it hadn't been. She'd put Daniel in an awkward position. Still, trying to apologize would only make it worse, wouldn't it?

The sound of a buggy coming up the lane did succeed in chasing the thoughts away. She leaned across the sink to peer out the window. It was Lydia, with Beth's niece Janie sitting beside her. She hadn't expected anyone tonight, but already Benjy was clattering down the steps, eager for company.

"Look, Mammi, it's Janie. Maybe she came to play with me."

"Maybe." Wiping her hands on a tea towel, she followed him to the door. "Lydia is there, too. Be sure you greet each of them."

She didn't have to worry about that, as Benjy hurtled himself first at Janie and then at Lydia, beaming with pleasure. Did that outgoing personality of his come from his father? A chill touched her. It was a wonderful trait, as long as it didn't lead him too far. Like James.

"It's wonderful gut to see both of you. But what—"

"There, I told you she'd forgotten," Lydia said. "You did, didn't you?"

Beth stared blankly, and Lydia laughed.

"It's the night our rumspringa gang is getting together at Esther Mueller's house, remember? Well, never mind. We'll be in plenty of time, and Janie is here to stay with Benjy."

"Yaay!" Benjy didn't hesitate to express his joy. He grabbed his cousin's hand. "Komm. We'll play a game, ain't so?"

Janie nodded, and they scurried toward the living room before Beth could object.

"I did forget." She turned back to Lydia. "Honestly, I think I'd rather not go. I've had a long day, and…"

"And you need to get out of the house and talk to some friends. If there's anything our gang can do, it's talk."

"But I really don't want to." She'd have to be firm, or Lydia would have her in the buggy before she knew it.

"But you really need to," Lydia countered. "Don't bother to tell me you weren't brooding, because I can see it in your face." She linked her arm with Beth's. "Is that the face you want your son to look at tonight? Komm, schnell."

Lydia's analysis was too accurate, and Beth stopped resisting. "All right, I'll go. But I warn you, I'm not going to be the life of the party."

"That's okay, so long as you're there." Lydia hustled her out to the buggy.

The sun was lingering at the top of the ridge, turning the valley a golden hue that looked like autumn. The chill in the air reinforced that thought. She'd always loved fall better than any season, but this year it threatened to be a melancholy time.

The buggy turned onto the main road and headed away from town toward the Mueller farm. Lydia swung to study her face. "Komm now. You may as well tell me."

"Tell you what?" She tried to sound as if she didn't know what Lydia was talking about, but it sounded hollow even to herself.

Lydia's gaze grew skeptical. Beth, unable to ignore that look, shrugged. "All right. If you must know, I heard something that upset me today at the store." She hesitated, wanting to tell it without getting into what had happened with Daniel.

"One of the drivers, an Englischer, asked where James was. And when I said he wasn't here any longer, he…" She seemed to run out of breath. "He said that some husband must have chased him out of town." She got it out in one breath.

Lydia didn't speak, but her hand clasped Beth's, and sympathy flowed from her in waves. "I'm sorry. He didn't know who you were. When he finds out, he'll feel like a monster."

"There's no reason he should ever find out," she said quickly. "I don't want to embarrass him. But it makes me think…" Her fingers tightened on Lydia's hand. "That's what everyone is saying, ain't so? Everyone knows what James was like."

"Not everyone." Lydia was trying to soften it, but that didn't help.

"Everyone who knows him." She had to accept it. "So they're all either feeling sorry for me or laughing at me. Which is it?"

"Ach, don't be so foolish," Lydia scolded. "Most people just recognized James's outgoing personality. As long as you didn't seem upset about it, no one else would take it that way."

"Obviously that driver did." Beth shook her head impatiently. "It doesn't matter, not for me. But Benjy— what if Benjy heard something like that about his father?" She tried to imagine dealing with that, trying to explain it to a four-year-old, but couldn't.

Lydia was silent as the buggy negotiated the turn into Mueller's lane. "He's not old enough," she said finally. "If he heard something, he wouldn't understand it, would he?"

"I guess not," she admitted. "Not now. But someday."

"I know you want to protect him." Lydia patted her

arm. "But when the day comes that he asks you about it…well, by then it should be easier."

Somehow Beth couldn't imagine the time when it would be easier, but she knew Lydia was trying to help, and she was thankful.

Chapter Six

Lydia's buggy stopped at the back door, where Esther's husband and their oldest boy stood waiting to take the horse and buggy. He greeted them with a grin.

"Are you two ready for a night of talking? I don't know how you can find so much to say to each other, that's certain sure."

"The same way you men find so much to say after worship or when you go to the hardware store," Lydia replied, never at a loss for words, as usual.

Beth, not so talkative, just smiled, following her.

But at the door, Beth hesitated, doubts assailing her. Was this really a good idea? Was it too soon to come back? She gave her black skirt a shake to fluff out the wrinkles. She wanted nothing so much as to be normal this evening, talking and reminiscing with her childhood friends. The black dress marked her out as different.

She couldn't retreat now, so she walked into the kitchen, where several of the gang were helping themselves to coffee. "Go on into the living room," Esther said, making shooing motions with her hands. "I'll bring dessert in when it's ready." She caught sight of Beth then and came toward her, wiping her hands on her apron.

"Ach, Beth, I'm wonderful glad you came. Lydia said she'd bring you, but I..."

"You thought I'd resist," Beth said, embracing her. "You know it's no use resisting when Lydia's decided you should do something."

"She's like a horse within sight of the barn." Esther grinned as she hugged her. "Get your coffee and head on into the other room. I don't know why everyone always wants to linger in the kitchen."

"Because it smells so gut," Beth replied, feeling more relaxed every moment.

"Because we like to get in your way," Lydia added.

Picking up their cups, they followed the sound of talk toward the front of the farmhouse.

Beth gave a quick look around. It seemed they were all present. There had been twenty girls in their original group, and every one of them had stayed here in the area. Except for her cousin Miriam, and Miriam was in Ohio helping her sister with a new baby and visiting her aunt and uncle there. She'd surely be home soon.

Beth found a seat next to Ella Esch. Beyond Ella was her twin, Della. The two of them had married the Esch brothers, second cousins of James, and now lived in two cottages on the Esch family's dairy farm. It wasn't all that unusual for two sisters to marry two brothers, but it certain sure added to the confusion, especially with such a common name as Esch.

Ella clasped her hand warmly. "We're wonderful glad you came. Since the accident—" She stopped, flushing a little, and then blurted out, "I told my Davey I didn't want him going out on that lonely road at night. I don't want to lose him."

No sooner had the words gotten out than Della started scolding, quickly echoed by everyone who was close enough to hear. Ella flushed bright red up to her hair and hid her face.

Beth sat perfectly still for a moment. That was it, and she hadn't realized it. The awkwardness with them wasn't just because she was a widow now. It was because they feared if it happened to her, it could happen to them.

"It's all right…" she began, only to be drowned out by Della's scolding.

"You are the most tactless person in the world." She looked as if she'd like to shake her twin the way she'd done when they were six. "Apologize to Beth."

"I'm sorry." Ella raised a tearstained face, and Beth reached out with a handkerchief to blot the tears away.

"It's all right, really." She gave Ella a quick hug. "I understand. And it's gut to remind our loved ones to be careful." She kept her voice calm and light, even though she was still shaking a little inside.

Still, she was just as glad it had happened. Poor Ella. Her habit of saying exactly what she was thinking had gotten her into trouble in school more times than they could count. But this time the fault, if that was what it was, had helped Beth understand what other women were feeling when they looked at her.

"None of us has changed, yah?" Beth looked around the circle of faces. She wanted to go on, wanted to say that the black clothing didn't change who she was inside, but she hesitated, afraid they wouldn't understand.

But her words had banished the awkward moment, and when Esther began forcing pieces of peach pie on them, they were quickly back to normal.

"What's happening with your cousin Miriam, Beth? We thought she'd be back with us by this month."

"She intended to come back by the time her sister's boppli was six weeks old, but the older children got some kind of a bug, and they've been sick one after another. So of course Miriam felt she had to stay."

Esther's eyes twinkled. "I thought maybe she'd met a wonderful nice man and was courting."

"Not unless she's keeping it a secret from us," Lydia said. "She'd better not be keeping secrets from her favorite cousins." She smiled at Beth, and it seemed the smile carried assurance. *You're doing fine, yah?*

The talk drifted to children, as it often did—the way little girls grew out of their clothes while the boys wore out of them, the need for a couple of new swings at the schoolyard, and the challenge of keeping the little ones from catching everything the older ones got.

"How is your little Benjy doing, Beth?" Della leaned toward her.

"He's doing fine. My niece Janie is with him now. She's willing to watch him while I'm at the store if I need her, although he seems happy enough at the store. I thought he might feel shy, but he enjoys it."

"Just like his daadi, then," Ella said. "James was always smiling in the store."

Beth froze for a moment, trying to hold a meaningless smile on her face. Was she imagining it, or had the other women frozen, too?

She looked down at the cup she still held before setting it carefully on the table next to her. All of them would have seen James at the store. Probably most of them had talked to him when she wasn't around.

How many of them had watched James flirting with other women? Had they been pitying her all this time?

Maybe it was worse. Maybe one of them had been the woman who'd written that note.

She was back in the trap, running around and around, searching for the truth. Wondering if she would ever know. Or if she could find peace without it.

Daniel glanced at the clock when he saw Beth and Benjy coming the next morning. They were about ten minutes later than usual, not that it mattered. He was happy to have her come whenever she could make it. Every day that passed seemed to make her more a part of the business.

"I'm sorry we're late." She glanced at the clock as he had. "I don't know why we couldn't get moving this morning."

"You're one of the bosses," he said lightly. "You can come whenever you want." His gaze fell on Benjy just as the boy gave a huge yawn and rubbed his eyes. Daniel chuckled. "I think I see why."

Beth's lips trembled on the verge of a smile. "It's not entirely his fault. I got together with my rumspringa gang last night, so Janie came to stay with him. And he always manages to get one more game or story out of his cousin Janie before she puts him to bed."

Benjy seemed to realize they were talking about him. "Cousin Janie likes to play games and tell stories," he protested.

"I know. I do, too. But bedtime is important."

"Especially when you're getting up to go to work in the morning," Daniel added, winking at Benjy to show that he was joking.

Benjy twinkled back, looking marginally more awake. "I should see what Timothy is doing," he said, and darted off toward the back of the store.

"Speaking of Janie, she's going to watch him a couple of mornings a week, so that Benjy won't be here every day." She glanced at him, as if wanting to see his reaction.

"We love having him here," Daniel protested, concerned about what was behind this decision. She wasn't regretting the idea of staying involved with the store, was she? His dismay at that was probably obvious to her.

She smiled, shaking her head. "You're very kind, but I think it's best if he has a break sometimes. And Janie's eager to have a job, so it works out all around."

He couldn't very well argue, but... "We'll miss Benjy when he isn't here. Timothy likes having somebody younger around." He grinned. "He's used to having young ones around. But sometimes I think he'd rather be an only one."

Beth chuckled, her eyes twinkling. "Isn't that always the case? I think being in the middle is best."

His heart warmed at seeing her looking so much like her old self. "Me, too. There's always plenty of room to distribute blame when somebody's in trouble. Whoever's oldest usually gets held responsible."

Her smile faded, and her face became thoughtful. "We don't know what it's like to be an only child, do we?"

She was thinking about James, he felt sure. He hesitated, leaning against the counter while he tried to make up his mind what to say.

"James seemed happy to be an only child," he commented finally.

"Yah." Trouble still darkened her eyes.

Clearly, he hadn't helped. "I used to think…"

"What?" Beth studied his face, as if trying to read more than he'd said.

"I kind of envied him. He didn't have chores to do, living in town like he did. My daad never ran out of jobs for us to do if he caught us wasting time." He smiled, remembering. "And his mamm didn't say no nearly as much as my mamm did."

"I don't suppose she did." Beth seemed to focus on her mother-in-law, and she wasn't smiling.

That didn't surprise him. Sarah Esch had always been one to fuss over a person, and as a mother-in-law, she'd fuss twice as much, he'd imagine. Beth wasn't one to like that.

Beth seemed to shake off thoughts of her mother-in-law. "I should get to work. I'll finish updating the inventory of canned goods I started."

He nodded, watching her go. There had been moments when the conversation had been as comfortable and relaxed as ever, but then he started feeling he hadn't been very helpful. There was something behind her troubled look, and he wasn't sure what it was. The truck driver's comments? Or something else?

His musing was interrupted by Benjy tugging at his pants. "Are we going to fix that step? You said I could help." Benjy fixed his wide-eyed gaze on Daniel.

The boy was not only smart and talkative. He was also determined.

"Yah, sure." It had to be done, so it might as well be now. "Komm, we'll get the tools."

Benjy skipped along beside him as they walked to the back door. "I like fixing things," he said. "Don't you?"

Daniel smiled at his enthusiasm. "Yah, I do. Especially when I have someone like you to help."

"Gut."

Once they'd reached the rickety step, he squatted down to examine it, amused when Benjy mimicked his motion, balancing on his heels and putting his elbows on his knees.

"See how the step is working away on this one side? This nail is loose, ain't so?"

Benjy wiggled it with a small finger. "Yah. We'll put a new one in, won't we?"

"We will," he agreed. "You hold the hammer while I get the nails out."

Benjy grasped the hammer with both hands, his small face intent and proud.

Daniel's heart warmed at the sight. Here, at least, was a way he could help.

To Beth's surprise, she and Benjy found her mother waiting on the back porch for them when they went home. Benjy rushed forward for a hug, and Beth wasn't far behind him.

"Ach, this is a nice surprise." She relished the feel of her mother's arms around her. "Will you stay for lunch?"

Mammi smiled, her blue eyes twinkling as she held up the basket she'd parked on the floor. "Better. I brought a picnic for the three of us."

Benjy was already bouncing with pleasure, and he tried to take the basket, but Beth forestalled him. "We'll need something to sit on, yah? You bring the rag rugs we keep in the back closet."

He darted off, and Mammi chuckled. "That boy has more energy than the two of us put together."

"Easily." She picked up the basket. "This is a nice idea. I was just thinking that I hadn't seen you since Sunday."

Her mother linked arms with her as Benjy hurried out, his arms loaded with the rugs. "It's time for a talk, ain't so?"

"What's in the basket, Grossmammi?" Benjy stretched himself on tiptoe for a moment, trying to see in, but a striped tea towel hid the contents.

"We'll see when we get to the picnic spot," she said, smiling so sweetly at him that Beth's heart warmed. "You remember where we went last time?"

Benjy nodded vigorously. "Up there." He pointed toward the orchard. "I'll put out the rugs."

The sight of him trying to carry the rugs and run at the same time had Beth smiling. No matter how many grandchildren she had, her mother had time and love for each one.

"I want to hear all about working at the store, but I guess we'd best feed this hungry boy first."

Mammi helped Benjy spread out the rugs. Sitting down, she took the basket and started lifting out food, putting it on the tea towel.

"Sandwiches with church spread." Benjy's eyes widened at his favorite—the spread of peanut butter and marshmallow cream that was so popular with the young ones. He looked as if he'd say more, but his mouth was quickly plugged with the sticky mixture.

Beth was glad to see that her mother had included meat and cheese sandwiches. She'd outgrown her love for church spread before she was out of her teens. Finding a spot on a rug, she relaxed, taking in the scent of apples that filled the air with its reminder of harvest. If she'd been blindfolded and brought here, she'd have known where she was without looking. No other place could smell quite this way.

Mammi began telling Benjy a story as they ate, and

Beth leaned back on her elbows, enjoying the warm fall afternoon. Off to the right from where they sat, she could see Daniel's family farm, with his mamm out in the backyard hanging up clothes. To the left lay her parents' farm, but the curve of the hill hid most of the house. Daadi was in the pasture next to the road, mending fence before any of the cows took a notion to go looking for greener grass.

The curve of the road bounded the property, and the store sat there, almost directly in front of her. With the ridge behind her, nearly everything she could see was her place in the world, and Benjy's. That was as it should be. Even fatherless, Benjy would grow up surrounded on all sides by people who loved him.

Benjy leaned across his rug to hug his grandmother. "Denke. That was a wonderful gut picnic."

She squeezed him back, smiling, and turned back to Beth as Benjy skipped off through the windfall apples. "It's hard to resist that little one. He has his daadi's charm." She paused for a moment. "But he has your heart for other people, too. He'll be all right."

"I'm not worried about that," Beth said quickly, sensitive on that subject.

"Komm, Beth." Her mother patted her hand. "That quality in James caused you sorrow sometimes, ain't so?"

She couldn't speak, because Mammi's words were too close to the bone.

Her mother didn't seem to expect an answer, going on. "I was worried from the first time I saw you were interested in him. He could smile and make a woman feel that she was important to him. But I thought he spread it around too much."

"Why didn't you say anything to me then?" She studied her mother's face, looking for an answer.

Mammi smiled a little sadly. "You were in love. You wouldn't have listened. Besides, I thought once you were married, maybe he'd save his charm for you. All I could do was pray that it was so."

Beth averted her gaze to study the pattern of faded colors in the rug. How had she not known that her mother had those reservations about her marriage? She began to think she had been blind when it came to James.

"So now all you can do is to forgive him if he hurt you." She reached out to touch Beth's chin, tilting it to see her eyes. "Have you been able to do that?"

Her mother didn't know how much she had to forgive, or how far James had strayed. And Beth couldn't tell her.

"I try, but it still bothers me some." It bothered her a lot, but surely it would get better soon.

"I knew there was something you weren't saying."

"How could I?" She desperately wanted this conversation over before she said something she shouldn't. "I can't talk about James's faults, especially now that he's gone."

"My poor Beth." Mammi patted her hand. "Peace will come, in God's own time."

"Until then…"

"Until then, you must pray to be able to forgive.

And you must do and say what you would if you really had forgiven."

She was silent, wrestling with it. "That sounds like you want me to pretend."

"It's not pretending," her mother said. "It's trusting the gut Lord to give you what you've asked. Will you try to do that?"

Beth brushed back a strand of hair pulled loose by the wind. Her fingers touched her kapp, with its constant reminder to pray.

"Yah," she said finally. "I'll try."

Chapter Seven

Janie arrived early the next morning, obviously looking forward to her new job. Benjy was delighted to see
her, but not so delighted to learn that he wasn't going
to the store this morning.

"But, Mammi, I'm a big help at the store."

Beth pulled her sweater on against the chill of the
fall morning, hoping to make the parting short and
sweet. "Of course you are. But we'll get along without
you for one day. And besides, Janie wants to play with
you. Maybe she'll even take you for a hike."

"Sure I will." Janie responded quickly. "Meantime,
why don't we go and gather eggs? Do you know where
the egg basket is?"

"Yah." He gave her a sidelong glance. "But the big
rooster…"

They both knew that Benjy was a little scared of
the rooster, who had a habit of lunging at intruders to
his kingdom.

"Tell you what," Janie said. "We'll take the broom,

and if he tries anything, we'll give him a gut swat. Okay?"

Benjy considered a moment, and Beth edged toward the door.

"Yah, okay." Benjy grabbed Janie's hand. "Bye, Mammi."

Relieved, she gave him a quick hug and slipped off, half expecting a call after her. But apparently Janie had things under control, and a glance over her shoulder told Beth they were off toward the chicken coop, carrying the broom and the basket between them.

Setting off down the lane alone felt odd. Since Benjy's birth, there had been few times that they'd been separated. Maybe this would be good for him. In two years, he'd be off to school, hard as it was to believe.

As for her—well, she was going to her job, and she felt a certain satisfaction in that fact. At first, she hadn't been able to imagine doing this, and she still remembered the fear she'd felt at Daniel's suggestion.

Smiling, she waved a bumblebee away from her face and watched it dive toward the asters along the fence. Working at the store had been even scarier than the belligerent rooster. Now she looked forward to it.

When Beth reached the front of the store, she paused for a moment, glancing at the displays in the two big windows. Would a person call them displays? Stacks of various canned goods didn't seem to her to be an attractive advertisement for the store.

How would Daniel react if she suggested doing something different? She could think of half a dozen things that would make the window more attractive.

Daniel had been fine with her helping around the store, but he might feel she hadn't been there long enough to change things. Still, her newfound confidence might be great enough to try. She began thinking about how to bring it up.

As soon as she entered, she spotted Daniel, his face clouded, striding toward her.

"I'm glad you're here," he said abruptly.

"I'm not late, am I?" She glanced at the clock to see she was right on time.

"No, not at all." He chased away the frown. "Sorry. I just heard that Anna is going to be late today, and I've got a shipment arriving in a couple of minutes and a couple other things to do in the back. But now you're here, you'll be able to mind the store."

Beth could sense that he was still concerned, and she made a guess. "Is there some problem with Anna?"

He gave her a rueful smile. "Just the usual one. Her father. Every once in a while, Hiram starts in on her about respecting your father and mother and how she should be doing more at home. I guess this was a bad morning—she stopped at the convenience store at the other end of town to call."

Beth's ready compassion went out to the girl. "That's foolish. After all, she's already working a full day here."

"And taking her paycheck home to her parents," he added.

She shook her head, praying she'd never be that sort of parent. "It's one thing to be strict about the Ordnung and another to be downright nasty. My parents managed, even with my brothers, to insist on right behavior without being so…"

"Nasty," he finished for her. "You had the right word to begin with. We were fortunate in our parents, ain't so?"

Beth nodded. "Yah, we were. They set a gut example, and they were firm but never unfair."

The buzzer went just then, announcing the delivery truck, and Beth hurried behind the counter. "You go on. I'll take care of things out here."

He flashed her the smile that crinkled his eyes. "I know you will."

Beth found herself dwelling on Daniel's words as he headed back to the storeroom. It sounded as if he found her a help. She didn't kid herself that she could do everything that James had done in the partnership, but she liked knowing Daniel appreciated her efforts. It might be easier than she'd thought to bring up changing the window displays.

The Englisch woman who'd been browsing at the far end of the store came toward the counter with a full shopping basket.

"Ready to check out?" Beth smiled at her, admiring the way her turquoise scarf contrasted with the dark red of her hair. Not many Amish had red hair, and if they did, it was usually a light carroty color. This red was as rich and dark as the sorrel gelding Daad had once owned.

"I suppose so." The woman looked at her questioningly. "You're new, aren't you?"

"I've only been working here for a short time." Beth

weighed the bag of apples the woman had picked out, tempted to tell her that they'd come from her own trees. "Did you find everything you were looking for?"

A frown creased the woman's smooth skin. "Not quite. I was hoping you might have a few quilted table runners in the craft section, but it's looking pretty bare right now."

In an instant, Daniel's voice slid into her mind, saying that maybe James had been going to visit some crafters the night he died. Her fingers shook, and she grasped the carton of eggs with both hands.

"Is something wrong?" The woman was looking at her strangely.

"No, not at all. My husband used to handle the craft section before he…before he passed away. We'll probably be getting some more things in soon, if you'd like to come back."

"I'm sorry." The woman looked horrified for a moment. "I didn't realize. It was your husband who had that buggy accident, then."

Beth nodded. She shouldn't have said anything, but it had been surprised out of her. And now that it was done, she couldn't help noticing that the woman was even more upset than she was.

It wasn't her fault. She couldn't have known that her words would have an effect on Beth.

"It's all right to mention him." Beth produced a smile, but her mind was working busily behind it. The woman was attractive—very much so—and not a lot older than Beth, although it was always hard to tell age in an Englisch woman.

She'd already told herself that the woman James had been seeing might have been an Englisch woman. He met all kinds of people in the store. Could this be the one?

She looked down to bag the woman's produce, glad she had an excuse not to look at her. She could hardly go around accusing other women of being involved with her husband.

She ought to say something. The customer would find it odd. But before she could speak, the woman had thrust the money at her and had seized her bags and gone.

Daniel had just finished unloading when Anna scurried in, averting her gaze in a way that said she didn't want to talk. Frustrated, he shook his head. Not that he wanted to interfere with Hiram Fisher's family, but Anna was a good, hardworking youngster and he hated to see her so upset.

He considered following her, trying to get her to talk, but she went straight to the counter to relieve Beth, and he gave it up, a little relieved. If anyone could get her to talk, Beth would do a better job than he ever could.

He saw them exchange a few words. Beth gave her a gentle pat on the shoulder, but Anna seemed to flinch away. As he'd feared, Anna was determined to keep her troubles to herself.

A few minutes later, Beth joined him in the back of the store. She cast a concerned look at Anna. "Someone should talk to Hiram."

"I doubt it would do much good."

When anger flashed in her eyes, he shook his head. "I know. I'd like to fix it, too. But I fear anything we might say to Hiram would make things worse."

The anger faded. "You're right, I suppose. At least she's here much of the time, instead of constantly under his eye."

"I never thought of the store as a haven, but you might be right." He kept his voice deliberately light. Beth had enough to deal with on her own without fretting over someone else.

He was rewarded with a hint of a smile. "Speaking of the store," she began, then seemed unsure how to continue.

"Yah?"

"Have you ever thought...well, of doing a sort of display in the windows?" Beth's voice faltered a little, as if fearing he'd be insulted.

Well, he wasn't—he was delighted. Beth was showing enough interest in the business to want changes. That meant she'd begun to consider it hers.

"I never thought of it." That was true enough. "It's a fine idea, but I wouldn't know where to begin. Do you have any ideas?"

"Actually, I have thought of a few things that would make it look brighter and more appealing. And maybe highlight some of the autumn fruits and vegetables."

"That sounds great." He'd have said that in any event, just to see her smile. "Why don't you take it on?"

Beth's green eyes lit with enthusiasm. She looked as if he'd given her a present. "I'd like that fine. Are you sure you don't mind?" Again that hint of apprehension in her voice made him want to chase it away.

"Mind? It's a great idea. Where should we start? You tell me what to do, and I'll carry things for you."

Apparently, that convinced her. She went to the window so quickly he had to hurry to catch up.

"I just thought of it this morning, so I don't have it all planned out yet. But I was thinking since autumn is coming on, we could arrange things that remind folks of that. A few pumpkins and cornstalks, maybe."

The pleasure in her face was enough to convince him to do whatever necessary to keep it there. "I'll bring the cornstalks in tomorrow. There are some dry ones in the lower field that haven't been cut. And what about maybe a pail or basket with winter squash and such?"

"Yah, gut. That way I can switch them out every day or so." She grasped a case of canned beans and started to pull it out of the window.

"Whoa. I'll move cases. You just say where." He reached past her to take the box, his hands brushing hers and sending a little flush of warmth up his arms. He pulled the box away quickly.

"I'm not that helpless." Her face lit with amusement. "Don't you remember how we used to load baskets of apples? I could do as many as you."

"I don't know about that." He climbed into the window, relieved to see that Timothy, whose job it was, had kept it clean. "But you weren't bad for a girl."

As they cleared out the window, preparing it for the transformation, Beth seemed happier than she had in a long time. Maybe it was partly the excitement of a new project combined with some easy chatter about old times. Reminiscing, even when she mentioned James now and then, came easily, and he encouraged it, searching his memory for happy times they'd shared.

With the last cardboard box removed, Beth looked around the space with satisfaction. "Gut. I have some of those old crates that my onkel used—they'd be just right to set things on."

"I remember them. Didn't we take some in to school for a spring program?" he asked, remembering. "And James jumped on one and broke it. I thought the teacher would be angry, but she didn't say a word." He shook his head. "He was the teacher's pet, ain't so?"

He glanced at Beth, but he didn't see the answering amusement he expected. "Yah." Beth's lips tightened. "James could always charm any woman."

If it helped, he'd slap himself for saying such a foolish thing. Clearly Beth hadn't forgotten the careless words the driver had spoken. And what must he do but say something that reminded her.

Above all else, he had to avoid letting her sense his own suspicions. "That was Teacher Emma, I'm afraid. She liked the boys better than the girls, I always thought." It was a foolish comment, he supposed, but he had to say something.

Her face tightened, and he knew she wasn't soothed.

"Did you notice the woman I was helping when you went to do the unloading?" Her tone was abrupt.

"I… I guess so. Red-haired, wasn't she? That's Mrs.

Philmont. She comes in pretty often for fresh produce. Why?"

Beth didn't meet his eyes. "She seemed a little odd when she realized who I was. I thought…well, maybe she was someone James liked to flirt with." She shook her head quickly. "Never mind. I'm sorry I said it. I can't go around wondering about every woman who comes into the store."

Daniel didn't know what to say. He'd give anything to be able to say that James never looked at another woman, but she'd know that wasn't true. James had always looked. Even when they were teenagers…

He tried to stop that line of thought, but it wouldn't be stopped. James had only had to look at a girl to melt her heart. Even Beth, the girl his best friend cared for.

The fault was his, not James's. If he'd spoken up sooner… But he hadn't, and he'd lost his chance with Beth. It had been too late for him a long time ago.

Beth found herself mulling over that conversation with Daniel as she clamped the food mill onto the kitchen table that evening. Lydia would be there any minute, and they were going to can a batch of applesauce with some of the McIntosh apples she'd picked. With Benjy visiting his grandmother, they'd be able to have a good talk.

Would she or wouldn't she tell Lydia about Daniel? There wasn't that much to tell, she assured herself… just the fact that she'd spoken more frankly with Daniel about James than she'd done with anyone else, even her mother.

She couldn't tell her parents. It would hurt them too much. And Lydia had found out just by being there.

But Daniel knew at least part of the problem because she'd turned to him in her pain, and he'd been there, comforting and sure. The kind of good friend who came along a few times in a lifetime.

She wondered at the amount of trust she'd shown in him, but she couldn't go back and undo it.

The sound of hoofbeats in the lane told her Lydia was there, and her heart lifted. She'd enjoy their time together, she decided, and not worry about what she should say and what she should keep quiet.

The inevitable chatter erupted as soon as Lydia reached the house. She came into the kitchen like a whirlwind, dumping down a box of canning jars, tossing her heavy sweater onto the hook and hugging Beth.

"I thought I wasn't going to get out of the house. My sister stopped by, for a minute, she said, but she wouldn't stop talking. And I wanted to get on with the dishes, but Mamm would think that was rude."

"It's all right. We have plenty of time. Is your sister okay? Which one?"

"Doris, of course. Who else would be complaining?" She grabbed a knife and started cleaning apples. "There's always something—if it's not the baby teething, it's the twins catching colds and her mother-in-law saying she should give them cod liver oil. It's enough to discourage you from getting married."

"You don't mean that," she said, thinking how popular Lydia had always been. Still, she'd never seemed to get serious about anyone.

"Maybe. Maybe not. I wish Miriam were home again," Lydia said, pausing in processing apples through the food mill. "It seems like forever since all three of us were together."

Beth nodded, picturing the youngest of the three cousins. Miriam's lively nature added spice to the time the three of them spent together.

"Soon, I hope," she said. "Her mamm mentioned that as soon as the last of the kinder got well, she'll head for home."

"We'd better wish none of those kinder catches another cold, or she'll be stuck there forever," Lydia grumbled.

Beth, knowing a bit more about the trials of having a sick youngster in the house, just shrugged. Lydia would learn when she had young ones of her own.

"Did I tell you who I saw in the store this week?" she asked, deciding to change the subject. "Aaron King came in with his bride." The King brothers were distant cousins, and everyone had been so pleased when Aaron came back where he belonged after too long in the Englisch world.

"How did they look?" Lydia gave her a mischievous look. "What do you think? Is Sally expecting yet?"

"What would your mother think?" she scolded. "An unmarried girl like you speculating on whether someone is pregnant?"

Lydia chuckled. "She'd think it was a sign I should be getting married myself. Come on, tell me."

"Don't you dare say I told you, but I think so. She

has that glow a woman gets. And with her sister-in-law expecting soon, too, they'll have a happy time."

"A busy time, anyway." Lydia began filling jars with the still-warm sauce. She glanced at Beth. "Are you longing to be back washing diapers and getting up in the night?"

Beth shrugged. "No point in thinking about it, is there? That part of life is over for me." The words sent a sharp pain to her heart. She tried not to think of it, but she did long for more babies. Grieving for James meant grieving for those babies who wouldn't be born.

"Nonsense," Lydia said sharply. "I suppose it's too soon now, but one day you'll marry again. It's the natural thing to do. Benjy needs a father, and you deserve to have a family to love."

She was shaking her head before Lydia finished speaking. "I can't. You of all people should realize that. How could I trust someone enough to marry again?"

"Ach, Beth, don't say that." Lydia left the applesauce to put her arm around Beth's waist in a quick hug. "James was the way he was, but every man isn't like that. There are plenty of gut, reliable men around. Daniel, for instance."

Beth pulled free of the hug. "Don't, Lydia. Daniel is a friend, but I couldn't feel that way about him."

Lydia didn't say anything for a moment, but Beth could feel Lydia's gaze on her, studying her. She seemed to be making up her mind what to say, but Beth knew better than to think she'd given up.

"I don't see why," she said finally. "Daniel has been your friend since childhood, and now he's your partner. Working together in the store, it's natural that you should grow even closer. Benjy likes him, doesn't he?"

She thought about Benjy's intent gaze following everything Daniel did when they worked together on some project around the store.

"Daniel's good with him," she admitted. "Benjy does like him, but that's not enough for marriage."

"You don't want Benjy to be an only child, like James was, do you?"

That stung, but she knew Lydia didn't mean to be unkind. "James's mother spoiled him, I suppose. But I won't do that." She wouldn't, would she? What if she was a little too protective at times? That was better than letting Benjy get hurt.

"Yah, she did. And other people did, too, I'm thinking." Lydia didn't seem inclined to give up on the subject. "Just because he could be such a charmer…" She hesitated, and then went on. "Well, I'm just saying that it would be gut for Benjy if you remarried. Give him another man to look up to. And you couldn't find a better man than Daniel, I'd say."

"Well, you've said it, but you don't have to keep repeating it." If that sounded tart, Beth couldn't help it.

"All right, I'll let it go for now," Lydia said. "But at least Daniel has helped you get out and do things. Look how pleased you were just at seeing Aaron and Sally. Being Daniel's partner is good for you."

Beth raised her eyebrows. "I thought you were letting it go," she reminded her. "I grant you everything you've said about Daniel. He's a fine, trustworthy man, but I'm still thinking I don't want to marry again."

Lydia began to protest, but Beth raised a hand to stop her. "If I change my mind about that, you'll be the first to know. In the meantime, just leave it, Lydia. Please."

"Sorry." Lydia grimaced. "I guess I got carried away. I just want you to be happy."

"I know." Beth's voice gentled. Lydia wanted what was best for her, but she didn't even know herself what that best was.

Daniel was the best of partners, and as Lydia pointed out, he was a good friend. He might not be exciting and charming like James was, but he was reliable and steadfast. She was blessed to have him in her life, but that didn't mean either of them were thinking about marriage.

And as for her instinct to confide in him…well, that didn't mean anything more serious, did it?

Chapter Eight

The rest of the week passed peacefully enough, with Benjy getting used to staying with Janie several days. He also went to James's mother for one morning and confided that it wasn't as much fun as staying with Janie.

Beth talked to him about the importance of appreciating what people did for him, although she couldn't help understanding. His grandmother loved him very much, but since she lived in a small house in town, there wasn't much for a little boy to do there.

The extra time allowed Beth to finish her decorations of the store windows without having Benjy want to climb into the windows, too. Now, standing back and looking at the finished product, she felt a sense of satisfaction, as well as feeling more a part of the business than she ever had.

"Beth…"

She turned to find Anna standing behind her, looking as hesitant as she always did. Beth's heart went out to her.

"Yah, Anna. Do you want me for something?"

"Nothing... I mean, I thought you could double-check yesterday's receipts for me before you go."

"For sure, though I think you're better at addition and subtraction than I am, ain't so?"

She accompanied Anna back to the counter, wondering a little that Anna had consulted her rather than Daniel. The receipts were always checked by two people, but this was the first time Anna had asked her. Was it a sign that she was getting used to Beth?

She couldn't help thinking that it would be good for Anna to have another woman to talk with, though she didn't suppose she could give any very useful advice.

Together they bent over the page. "We got so busy just before closing that I was in a rush." Anna gave her an apologetic glance.

"It's all right. We know it's important that you get home on time or your father will worry." Though *worry* probably wasn't the right word.

"Denke," Anna murmured. "I... I don't want to disappoint Daniel. He and...and James were so kind to me."

Poor child, she didn't seem to have much kindness in her life. Still, just the fact that she was working in the store made it more likely she'd find someone to love. Preferably a young man strong enough to stand up to her father, she amended.

"You're a big help," she said. "James often said what

a gut worker you are." That was stretching the truth a bit, but she felt sure he'd said it at least once or twice.

"He did?" Her face lit. "Denke."

As Anna turned quickly back to the accounts, Beth decided that was all the progress she'd be able to make today. Still, it was good to get that far with someone as shy as Anna.

"There, absolutely right," she said a few minutes later. She glanced at the clock. "I had best get those few groceries I wanted and be off home before it starts to rain." The clouds had been darkening for the past hour.

Anna hurried to pick up the bags she'd left behind the counter, and Beth took them in her arms. Her pantry was well stocked, but there was always something she needed, even so.

Daniel hadn't come back from deliveries yet, but she was comfortable leaving Anna in charge. If the threatening rain came, business would be quiet, anyway.

She made her way out the back door, only to find that the rain had arrived. She stood for a moment, debating. She wouldn't melt if she got a little wet, but the groceries might not fare so well.

Just as she decided to leave them until tomorrow, Daniel's buggy came around the store. He pulled up by the steps.

"You need a ride home, ain't so? Let me take those." He jumped down and relieved her of the grocery bags.

A surge of pleasure went through her at the sight of his smile and the sound of his voice. Because she didn't want to walk in the rain, she assured herself.

"It's been looking like it'll rain all day, and if I'd left a few minutes earlier, I'd have missed it."

"Or you'd have been halfway home and gotten soaked." Daniel extended a strong hand to help her up to the seat, and she smiled her thanks.

"Well, you were right on time to save me," she said lightly. "You finished the deliveries?"

"Yah, all done. Joshua Miller is sinking, so his daughter said. I passed the bishop going in as I came out."

"Ach, I'm so sorry for her. She'll miss him." It wouldn't be appropriate to feel sorry for Joshua. He'd had a long life, and when the Lord took him, it would be a relief from pain and a joy to him.

Daniel nodded. "Emma will miss him, despite the difficult time she's had taking care of him. Death wipes out the trouble folks have caused, I guess."

She couldn't help wincing. "Not always."

He swung to face her, drawing up the horse. "Ach, Beth, I'm sorry. That was thoughtless. But no matter what James might have done or what I suspected—"

Daniel came to an abrupt stop, and she saw the guilt wash over his face. Saw it and in an instant feared she knew what had caused it.

"What do you mean? Suspected what? You know, don't you? James was carrying on with someone, and you knew."

"No, no, I didn't." He reached for her hand, but she pulled it away.

"Don't tell me lies." Anger carried her on so strong

a wind that she couldn't think straight. "Tell me. What do you know? Who was the woman?"

"Beth, stop. It's not like that. I don't know anything, not for sure. I just thought that there was something…" He shook his head, as if angry at himself. "Look, it wondered me. Sometimes he left early—drove off without telling me where he was going."

The anger faded slowly, and she tried to hang on to it. It was better to be angry than to let the pain have free rein. She'd known, hadn't she? The note had told her so. But Daniel…

"You lied to me." The anger surged back. "I trusted you. I believed you when you said it was just James's way to chat with all the women."

"I didn't lie. I didn't really know anything. I might have suspected, but I couldn't condemn a friend based only on suspicion."

"I thought I was your friend." She threw the words at him and swung around. All she could think was to get out of the buggy, to walk away and never have to look at Daniel again.

He grabbed her wrist, holding it firmly. "What are you doing? You can't get out in the rain."

"I'd rather get soaked than talk to you any longer."

His face paled, but he picked up the lines with his left hand and set the horse moving. "I won't say anything. You'll be home in an instant."

It would take an undignified tussle to get out here. She closed her hands over the edge of the seat, staring straight ahead. If he said another thing…

But Daniel was true to his word this time. He

stopped the buggy at her porch. She jumped down before he could move to help her, snatched her bags and fled into the house.

Somehow Daniel managed to keep his face normal during the afternoon, although he saw Anna give him a wondering look a time or two. Timothy noticed nothing, of course. He was as oblivious of other people's feelings as most teenage boys, but at the moment, Daniel was just as glad. At least Anna wouldn't say anything, no matter how much she might wonder.

He might be able to hide his feelings from other people, but not from himself. How could he have been so careless? He should have known that Beth was too sharp and knew him too well to let any slip get by her. He'd doomed any chance he might have had with Beth, and he'd put the future of the store in jeopardy. That didn't mean anywhere near as much as the fact that he'd hurt Beth and let her down.

The ironic part of it was that he still didn't know anything for sure about James. Had he been involved with another woman? He wanted to reject that idea— wanted to be ashamed that he even suspected it. But he couldn't. Maybe he knew, in some deep, unacknowledged part of his soul, that James could have done it. Whether he did or not…

Now that he thought back over what he'd said and what Beth had said, he started to wonder. How had Beth jumped to the conclusion so quickly? Surely that foolish comment by the trucker hadn't been enough to make her think that.

It didn't really matter how it had all happened. He had to do something. He had to talk to Beth, to beg her forgiveness and to pray she had it in her heart to forgive. No matter what she said to him, he deserved it.

He stayed on at the store after closing, busying himself with one chore after another. There was no sense in trying to have a conversation with Beth until she'd put Benjy to bed.

Finally it seemed late enough to make that likely. The gentle glow of autumn was fading into dusk as he walked quickly down the lane. He tried to form an opening sentence in his mind, but everything he thought of seemed too feeble to convince anyone.

It wasn't until Daniel neared the house that it occurred to him that Beth might have visitors. He couldn't say any of the things he needed to say with others there. Beth might not let him say them if she were alone, either. Practically the last words she'd spoken to him commanded him not to speak to her.

His effort to come up with a good opening line was unsuccessful, but at least there was no sign of anyone else as he approached the kitchen door. He hesitated a moment, breathed a silent prayer and knocked.

From beyond the door came the sound of footsteps. He saw the knob start to turn and then stop.

"Who is it?" Beth was either being cautious or else she suspected it was he.

"Beth, please let me in. I must speak with you. You have to hear my explanation."

"No. I don't." The words were implacable, but he

didn't hear her move away, and that gave him a whisper of hope.

"No, you don't have to," he agreed. Demanding wasn't the way to do this. "But I'm praying you'll let me say how wrong I was and how sorry I am."

Nothing but silence came from the other side of the door. The cold of despair settled into him. She would never forgive him.

The knob rattled. Slowly the door opened. Beth stood in the opening, her face pale and rigid. Then she stepped back wordlessly to let him in.

The house was silent. Benjy must be in bed, or he'd come rushing to see who was there.

Beth closed the door and folded her arms as if she were cold. "A few minutes. That's all."

He nodded. "Please, try to believe I was trying to do my best for you and Benjy." Seeing a retort forming in her expression, he hurried on. "I didn't know. I still don't know, not for sure. I'd started to be suspicious, that's all. I didn't want to believe it."

She didn't speak, but she gave a slight nod, and he felt encouraged. She must know what that was like. How did you believe that a person you cared deeply about could commit such a wrong?

She still didn't speak, and he knew he'd have to explain more fully.

"James...well, James always had a way with him. All the women liked him. Not just young women, but little girls and old women, too. I was used to it. I never suspected..."

He let that trail off. Maybe if he'd noticed, if he'd

taken it more seriously, he could have headed it off before James did something wrong.

"Maybe a month or two before his accident, I noticed he started leaving earlier. Or he'd come in to do inventory in the evening and make an excuse to leave after an hour."

Now for the hardest part. "It wondered me. I didn't want to think it. It was like a betrayal of my friend. But finally I couldn't hold it back. I had to speak. I told him my suspicions."

Beth didn't move, but her fingers dug into her arms hard enough to leave marks. He thought she was trying to shield herself from what she feared was coming.

"At first he tried to laugh it off."

Beth finally moved, maybe wanting to postpone the inevitable. She took a few steps and grasped the back of a kitchen chair.

"That last night..." His throat tightened, and the words came out hoarsely. "I tried again. I let him know I didn't believe him. He got angry. He stamped out. A few hours later I heard about the accident."

Beth sagged as if her bones had turned to water. Galvanized, he caught her before she could fall and lowered her into the chair. Why hadn't he realized... he shouldn't have told her that way. But she wouldn't settle for anything else.

He bent over her. "Just sit here. I'll get you water." Not waiting for a response, he grabbed a glass and splashed water into it, sloshing some onto the floor as he took it to her.

She tried to hold the glass, but her hands shook. He

clasped it in his and raised it to her lips. She gulped it down as if thirsty, but then in a moment she pushed it away, straightening in the chair.

"Enough," she murmured. "I'm all right. Sorry."

"My fault." He sank into the chair next to her. "Beth, please understand. James was gone, and you didn't seem to suspect anything. How could I tell you then? It would have hurt you to no purpose. I wanted to protect you and Benjy. If I was wrong, I'm sorry."

She shook her head slowly. "I understand. But I'd rather have the truth."

They sat silently. Daniel felt empty. He'd told her everything he knew. He couldn't do more.

After a bit, his mind started to work. He went back over everything they'd said to each other about James, and he saw something he'd wondered about.

He straightened, staring at Beth. "You suspected, didn't you? Not just because of what the driver said about James. You already thought something was wrong, didn't you?"

Beth looked at him, her green eyes darkening as if night was falling.

"Yah. I did." Beth seemed to come to a decision. "Wait here."

She walked to the hallway, and he heard her light footsteps going up the stairs. He stood where he was, wondering what was coming and how he could deal with it. He owed something to James as his friend, but even more to Beth, who was hurting so much.

It took Beth only a few moments to retrieve the note from its hiding place in her bedroom. She hesitated, holding it by the edges. She disliked even the feel of it against her fingers.

Perhaps if she'd burned it the day she'd discovered it, she'd have been able to forget, but it had been impossible. At first, she'd tortured herself by reading it over and over, trying to tease some meaning or identity from it.

Since she'd become so involved in the store, the power of that piece of paper had lessened. She hadn't looked at it in days, and she didn't want to see it now. And most particularly she didn't want to show it to Daniel.

There was no getting out of it now. She'd given too much away to keep it a secret now. Besides, she owed him the truth. He'd been open with her.

It couldn't have been easy for Daniel to tell her about that last conversation he'd had with James. She'd had no trouble recognizing the guilt and pain in his eyes when he'd spoken. After all, she'd felt the same herself—regretting every sharp word or thought of their marriage.

Refusing to let herself delay any longer, she marched back downstairs and into the kitchen. Dropping the note in front of him, she slipped back into the chair she'd vacated.

"I found this about a month after James died." She struggled for a second and then blurted out the rest of it. "Lydia had come over to help me get his clothes ready to give away." She felt again the aversion she'd felt that day. "I didn't want to, but she pushed me into it. I found the note in his drawer of the chest upstairs."

Daniel had read it by this time, and his forehead was knotted into a frown. "You're thinking it referred to that last night, but it might have been something old—some girl who had a crush on him."

He was trying to find an alternate explanation, just as Lydia had at first. She shook her head.

"No. I'd been in that drawer just a couple of days earlier. And look at it. It's not old."

Given his own suspicions, Daniel seemed to be having difficulty accepting the proof. Beth could almost see his internal struggle, and the moment in which he accepted it.

Daniel nodded slowly, his jaw hardening. "Yah. You're right."

He looked at her, studying her face so intently that she seemed to feel the touch on her skin. "This shows us what the woman felt about James. But not what James felt about her."

"It doesn't excuse him." Her voice was tart.

"No, it doesn't." Daniel folded the paper so that the words were hidden. He held it up between his fingers. "What are you going to do with this?"

"I don't know." She wavered, unsure.

"Wouldn't it be best to destroy it? You wouldn't want Benjy ever to see it."

"No, but..." She reached out and took it from him. "I'll burn it. But not now. I'm not ready yet."

Resentment rose in her. Daniel had said very little, but she knew he thought the note was better destroyed. Did he think her jealous or vengeful for hanging on to it? Maybe he did, and maybe he was right. She just knew she wasn't ready.

Daniel seemed to recognize the depth of her feeling. He put his hand over hers, and she felt compassion and understanding flow through the touch, finding its way to her heart. He wanted to protect her, much as she wanted to protect Benjy.

For the first time in too long, healing began, very slowly, to make its way through her. Gratitude welled in her heart. Without volition, her hand turned in his until they were palm to palm, clasped snugly. Beth didn't try to figure out what it meant. She just sat still, accepting.

Chapter Nine

"I'm going with you this morning, Mammi, ain't so?" Benjy was eager to firm up his plans for the day as he hopped down from his seat at the breakfast table.

"That's right." Beth hesitated, wondering if she was doing the right thing by taking him to work with her. Was it better than leaving him with Janie or worse? There didn't seem to be any guidelines that fit her situation, making her feel guilty either way.

"You like going to the store, don't you?" she asked.

"Yah, for sure." He gave a little hop that said he was eager to get started. "Daniel said I could help him today."

Beth felt an interior tremor at the mention of Daniel. The memory of what had happened between them the previous night was too fresh. She still hadn't managed to decide how she felt about it.

"What are you going to do?" It was cowardly to avoid saying his name. She'd best get herself together before they left for the store.

"Make a new shelf in the office. That's what Daniel said. He said we could make it in a jiffy."

She'd noticed her son was prone to quote Daniel several times a day now. "That will be wonderful gut. We need more space."

Benjy stopped his energetic hopping and stood still, seeming deep in thought. "Daniel's gut at making things." He paused, then looked up at her, his blue eyes wondering. "Was Daadi gut at making things?"

Beth's breath caught. She'd warned herself that one day Benjy would start asking questions about his daadi. She just hadn't expected it now. Should she simply answer, or did he need more assurance about his father?

"Daadi didn't make a lot of things at the store," she said carefully. "Daniel did that, and Daadi was gut at other things, like taking care of the customers. That's why they were partners…they each did something the other didn't."

She waited, watching his small face. Did he need more than that?

But she couldn't read any doubts in his eyes. He nodded as if satisfied and skipped toward the hall. "Hurry and get ready, Mammi. We need to get to work."

That startled a laugh from her. Where had he picked up that phrase? Well, it was true enough.

"As soon as I finish the breakfast dishes, we'll go. Did you make your bed yet?"

"I will." He darted off, and his feet thudded on the stairs.

Beth shook her head. One small boy could certainly make a lot of noise. And ask a lot of questions.

She wasn't sure how she felt about his growing closeness to Daniel. But it was natural, she supposed. In the past week, he had spent more time with Daniel than with his grandfather or his uncles. And there was never a need to worry when he was with Daniel.

Her thoughts slipped back to the previous night. She'd been so determined to hold on to her anger with him, but she hadn't been able to. She had understood him too well for that. He'd been torn by his long friendship with James fighting against his growing suspicions.

She would have been as well, if she hadn't found out in such a devastating way. The note had left no room for doubt.

The note. Daniel obviously thought it best destroyed at once. And he'd been right about the dangers of anyone else seeing it. If Benjy ever learned about his father's failing, it shouldn't be that way.

Or any way at all, if she could manage it. Lydia and Daniel were the only ones who knew, except for her. And the unknown woman.

Maybe Daniel had been right. There was no reason to keep it, and every reason to destroy it. Quickly, before she could change her mind, Beth retrieved the note from the drawer where she'd hidden it after Daniel left. Striking a match, she held it over the sink and lit the edge of the paper.

It burned quickly, the words disappearing into the flame, then the whole paper crumbling into ash. She turned on the faucet and washed the ash down the drain.

There. It was done. She wouldn't torment herself with it again. It was time to start looking toward the future, not the past.

Benjy galloped down the stairs and into the kitchen and stopped to sniff. "It smells like burning, Mammi."

"I guess it does." She kept her face away from him as she took her sweater from the hook and pulled it on. "It was just a little bit of trash. Komm, let's go to work."

The lane was still damp after yesterday's rain, and rain had brought down a fresh drift of leaves, as it always did. The season was moving on quickly, and it would soon be time for cider-making if she intended to do it this year.

That was one of the few orchard chores James had enjoyed, probably because they always had a group of people there to help and it always turned into a work frolic. Everyone brought something to share for supper, and they all had to try the fresh golden cider.

Beth struggled with the idea for a few minutes but then glanced at Benjy. He'd love it, even if he didn't remember it from last year.

She should mention it to Mamm and Daad, and together they'd pick a date. She couldn't stop doing it just because it reminded her of James.

A burst of wind swept them along with some bright yellow leaves, and they hurried into the store, laughing a little. "We beat the wind here," Benjy crowed, and trotted toward the back, where she could spot Daniel opening a carton.

Instead of heading in that direction, she paused at

the counter to exchange greetings with Anna, who was smiling as she watched Benjy.

"I tell him not to run indoors, but it doesn't seem to stick," she said.

She scanned Anna's face with the usual concern, but she actually looked better this morning. She didn't have the pallor she sometimes did. Maybe things were better at home. Beth said a quick prayer that it was so.

"Ach, no one cares that he runs here," Anna said. "We all love him."

It was the most personal thing Anna had ever said to her, and Beth's heart warmed. If she could grow closer to the girl, she might be able to help her.

"That's gut of you to say. But we all have to learn manners, ain't so? The trouble is that he usually makes me laugh just about the time I should be correcting him."

Anna was still watching Benjy. "He looks just like his daadi." Her words came out in a whisper, as if she were talking to herself, and then she seemed to hear what she'd said. She flushed, tears welling in her eyes. "I'm sorry. I shouldn't have said…"

"It's all right. It's gut for Benjy if people talk normally about his father." She reached out, thinking to comfort the girl with a pat on the shoulder, but Anna winced away.

"I… I should go and help Timothy." She scurried off.

Beth moved behind the counter. The poor girl had embarrassed herself, thinking she'd said the wrong thing. She remembered that stage where she'd wavered between being a child and a grown woman. It wasn't easy for anyone.

Daniel eyed Beth cautiously while he welcomed Benjy, pleased that the lad immediately started helping him unpack the carton. Beth seemed occupied with Anna, and as far as he could tell, she hadn't looked in his direction at all.

Was she angry with him about last night? He'd thought they'd parted with forgiveness on both sides, but maybe she'd regretted letting him comfort her. Or she might think he'd gone too far in saying she should get rid of that note. It wasn't his business to advise her to do something she didn't want to do.

The note had shocked him, and he could easily imagine the impact it had made on her, fresh from mourning her husband's death. A flicker of anger went through him. James should have had better sense. He'd been wrong to be seeing another woman, but if he'd been determined to sin, he might at least have destroyed that note and saved Beth a great deal of pain.

He'd been mad at James a number of times when they were young. That was only natural—kids fought and made up again, sometimes resorting to a shove or two. Still, he'd never felt as disappointed or as angry as he did now. How could anyone fortunate enough to have won Beth for his wife even look at anyone else?

Benjy tugged at his sleeve, and he realized the boy had been asking him something.

"Aren't we going to build the shelf today? I told Mammi, and she said that was gut." He tilted his face, obviously considering something. "Maybe she really needs it."

"I'm sure it will make her happy if we build it," he said gravely. "Let's break down this box and put it in the storeroom, and then we can get started."

Benjy, like any boy, enjoyed jumping on the box to flatten it. Even though it was now taller than he was, he carried it to the storeroom, talking all the time.

"I told Mammi that you were gut at making things. She said that Daadi was gut at other things."

"That's true." He held the storeroom door while Benjy slid the box through. "That's why we were partners."

"That's what Mammi said." Benjy beamed with satisfaction. He carried the box over to the right stack.

It was high enough that Benjy couldn't reach the top, so Daniel lifted him. The boy felt ridiculously light, and a wave of affection surged through him. He'd always been fond of Benjy, but since he'd been coming to the store, Daniel's feelings had grown deeper. If he could help it, Benjy wouldn't miss any of the care he needed. After all, there were some things only a man could teach a boy.

"Gut job," he said, setting Benjy down.

Benjy stood for a moment, eyeing the stack of cardboard. "Are you going to have a big fire with the boxes?"

He shook his head. "We keep them here, and anyone who needs boxes to pack things in can come and take as many as they want."

"Mammi was burning some trash this morning," Benjy volunteered. "She did it in the sink. I thought she should burn it outside."

"It must have been something very small." Something the size of a piece of folded paper.

Benjy didn't seem inclined to talk about it. "Are we going to build the shelf now?" He looked up at Daniel, his eyes filled with eagerness. "I want to learn how, so I can help."

"We'll get the tools and start, okay?" His mind wasn't on carpentry. Instead, he'd focused on the fact Benjy had innocently let slip.

Maybe he shouldn't have listened, but how could he help it? And had Beth been burning that note this morning?

He glanced across the width of the store to where Beth was helping a customer pick out a pumpkin. She was smiling, looking perfectly normal. In fact, she might be looking a little more at ease than she had in a long time.

If she had burned that note, he could only be thankful. No doubt he should have kept his opinions to himself. Still, she'd shown it to him. She wouldn't have done that if she hadn't wanted to hear what he had to say.

Daniel's stomach still turned queasy at the thought of it. Even if the note was gone now, the words were engraved on his mind. And, he didn't doubt, on Beth's, as well.

He'd thought it would be far better for Beth if she could forget about knowing who was going to meet James that last night. She'd have to forgive, no matter who it was, but that wouldn't be easy. *Forgive if you would be forgiven.* The Lord hadn't left any room for evasion in the words. He, too, had to forgive. James had hurt him, too, although not in the grievous way he'd caused pain for Beth.

She hadn't looked at him, he told himself as he and Benjy headed into the office with the toolbox. That didn't mean anything. She might not have noticed him. But he'd like to find out what she was thinking.

With the materials already gathered for adding the shelf, it wasn't going to take long. The challenge was to find something Benjy could do.

But Benjy was easy to please. Standing on a chair, watching intently, he grinned as they finished screwing in the second bracket.

"We did it," he exclaimed, so happy that Daniel had to grin back at him.

"We still have to put the shelf on," he cautioned. "Shall we try it?"

Benjy nodded. He seemed to hold his breath until the shelf was fixed into place. "There!" He paused. "If I learn a lot, will I be a gut partner, like Daadi?"

He hadn't expected the question, and it struck him right in the heart. "I think you'll be a very gut partner one day. Let's go tell your mammi."

Grinning, Benjy bolted across the office and on toward his mother. Daniel followed more slowly. Did he dare to bring up what Benjy had said? Probably not, but he longed to know.

Beth greeted him with a smile. "I understand you and your helper finished the new shelf."

"That we did. Is Benjy going to show it to you?"

"That's why he's pulling on my hand." She glanced at her son. "Just wait a minute," she told Benjy. "I have something to say to Daniel. You go ahead, and I'll be there in a minute."

Benjy let go and scooted off at his usual trot, and Beth looked at Daniel. "Denke, Daniel. I'm sure it takes longer when he helps, but he does love it."

He shrugged. "It's nothing." He'd do far more for Beth and her son if he could.

Beth hesitated a moment, glancing away as if she didn't want to meet his eyes. "I wanted to say… I took your advice. It's gone."

Unable to help himself, he clasped her hand for a second. "I'm glad."

Beth looked fleetingly into his face and then hurried after her son.

Standing there, seeming to feel the warmth of her hand still in his, Daniel faced the truth. He loved Beth. It might never come to anything but friendship, but he loved her.

Benjy was skipping alongside Beth as they headed for home later, making her feel she'd like to skip, as well. She seemed inexpressibly lighter, and she had no idea why.

She swung Benjy's hand, loving the way his fingers tightened on hers and the sweet expression in his soft, round face as he looked up at her.

"What makes you want to skip?" she asked.

His forehead crinkled as he considered the question.

He took another skipping step, and then his forehead cleared and his eyes lit. "I know. Because I feel happy, and when I skip, I get more happy."

Laughter bubbled up in her. "Gut. I'm glad you feel happy. I'll have to try that—maybe it will make me happier, too."

"Aren't you happy, Mammi?" With a quick change, his face turned serious.

"For sure I am." She scooped him into her arms for a hug. "Because I have you, and you make me happy all the time."

"Even when I'm naughty?"

"Even then," she assured him. And she knew just as suddenly why she felt so much freer. She'd resolved to turn away from the past and focus on their future—hers and Benjy's. No doubt she'd falter sometimes, but at least she was looking in the right direction.

Benjy tugged at her hand. "Skip with me."

Laughter bubbled up in her, and together they began to skip toward the house. Benjy had been right. Skipping did make her feel happier.

They were laughing and breathless when they reached the porch. Trying to catch her breath, Beth glanced at the door and found her mother-in-law looking back at her.

Sarah's expression sobered her instantly. It said she didn't approve—whether of the laughter or the skipping, Beth wasn't sure.

She forced herself to smile. "Look, Benjy. Here's your grossmammi come to see us."

Benjy scurried to hug his grandmother, and Sarah's disapproval transformed into a look of indulgent affection and pride. She pushed open the screen door and bent for a hug.

"Ach, there's my sweet boy. I'm sehr glad to see you."

When the hug went on a little too long for Benjy, he started to wiggle. Going to the rescue, Beth grasped the door to usher them inside.

"Sarah, this is such a nice surprise. If I'd known you were coming today, we could have come home a little earlier from the store."

"I didn't know myself." Sarah smoothed Benjy's silky-soft hair down where it tended to curl at the sides. "Myra Miller had to pick something up at her brother's place, so I said I'd ride along. I thought I could get some apples from you."

"For sure," Beth said, thankful she'd cleaned the kitchen up before they'd left. "Will you have lunch with us?"

"Better not." Sarah glanced at the clock. "We'd best get the apples so I'm ready when Myra comes back."

Myra, as Beth well knew, was Sarah's closest friend. Also a widow, she lived less than a block away from the cottage where James had grown up. An unstoppable talker, Myra was, and Beth had sometimes wondered how the two of them heard the other when they talked simultaneously.

Lifting a basket from a hook in the mudroom, Beth handed it to Benjy. "Let's pick them now. Would you like McIntosh or Red Delicious?"

"McIntosh, please. Then I'll make apple dumplings for when Benjy comes to visit me tomorrow. And maybe one or two of the Delicious."

Benjy was already scurrying out the door with the basket. "I'll get them," he called.

"Now, you wait until we get there before you start picking," Sarah said, hurrying after him.

"It's all right. He knows which ones to pick." Beth fell into step with her.

"But he might get hurt." Sarah gave her a look that suggested she was a negligent mother.

"I'm sure he'll be fine." After all, Sarah had lost her only son. She was bound to be feeling overly worried about her only grandson.

They walked in silence for another few steps, but Beth sensed Sarah had more to say.

Sure enough, Sarah emitted a sigh. "You know I'm not one to interfere," she began, "but I really have to caution you." She shook her head. "When I saw you running and laughing down the lane…don't you realize anyone might have seen you? And in your black dress, too."

Beth didn't know whether she felt more annoyed or more guilty, and she tried to compose herself before replying. "I'm sorry, Sarah. Perhaps it did seem frivolous, but Benjy was in such a happy mood that I wanted to encourage him." She tried to say more, but her throat seemed tied up in knots.

She certainly couldn't say anything about her own feeling of relief. Sarah wouldn't understand without knowing of James's failing, and she was determined that Sarah never would. That was the best thing she could do to protect her mother-in-law, and she'd keep that secret no matter what.

A glance at Sarah told her that she was near to tears. "Yah, for sure Benjy comes first. I just wouldn't want anyone to think you weren't properly mourning my son. It's important what others think of you. It reflects on James."

All Beth could do was nod and keep silent. There didn't seem to be any appropriate response that was also truthful.

"Well, let's forget it," Sarah said. "I'm sure you'll think again another time."

Sarah's attention was diverted by the sight of Benjy perched in the crotch of the biggest McIntosh tree, and she rushed toward him, uttering cautions and insisting he hang on until she could lift him down.

Benjy assumed his mulish expression, knowing that he was allowed to climb that high alone. In a moment he'd be telling his grandmother so. Murmuring a silent prayer for patience, Beth went in pursuit of Sarah, preparing to intercede and knowing it wouldn't be welcomed by her mother-in-law.

A memory popped to the front of her mind—Daniel's firm, quiet voice countering her objections to letting Benjy help that first day at the store. He'd been right, and she knew that now, but she doubted Sarah would ever admit to being overprotective, either toward Benjy or toward James.

Chapter Ten

❦

The next afternoon Beth and Benjy walked down the street toward Sarah's cottage. Sarah would be looking forward to his arrival. She glanced down at Benjy. For some reason, he seemed to be dragging his feet.

Familiar doubts nagged at her. Should she have left him with Janie this morning, knowing he'd be going to his grandmother's this afternoon? He was only four. Maybe all of the changes in his life were too much. Maybe he needed her with him more, not less.

As if he felt her gaze, Benjy looked up at her, his straw hat slipping on his soft corn-silk hair. Smiling, she straightened it.

He shook his head, obviously not caring if his hat was crooked. "What are you going to do this afternoon, Mammi?"

"I'm going to stop and see your other grossmammi. And *my* grossmammi, too."

Benjy puzzled over that for a moment and grinned when he got it. "I have an extra grossmammi, ain't so?"

"You do. We have lots of family around us."

"Yah. It's nice," he said. Then a cloud came over his face. "I wish I could go with you. It's more fun at the farm, especially if my cousins are there."

She could understand his feelings, but she couldn't let him have favorites among his grandmothers. "Your cousins are at school now, remember? And even if they weren't, you have to remember that different people live differently. When you're a guest, your job is to fit in."

Benjy nodded, but he still looked mopey. Even while she debated about whether she should say something more, he looked up with the smile that was so like James's.

"I'll behave, Mammi. And Grossmammi made me apple dumplings."

Apparently, the way to Benjy's heart was through his stomach. As long as he was good, she'd take it. Time enough for him to learn to be a gracious guest for the sake of kindness.

Sarah was waiting, opening the door as they went up the short walk to the cottage that had been her and James's home since before her husband died. As always, it looked spotless and tidy, the small patch of grass trimmed and the chrysanthemums along the porch tied to stakes so they wouldn't sprawl.

"Benjy!" Sarah held out open arms for a hug. "Komm in. I'm happy to see you." She glanced over his head at Beth. "I'll bring him home by suppertime, yah?"

Beth nodded. "Denke. Have fun, Benjy. I'll see you later."

He waved, seeming already lured by the scent of apple dumplings, and she chased the guilt away firmly. Benjy was all right. And she was doing the best she could with each new day.

It was a short walk back to the lane that curved behind her place to the farm where she'd grown up. The fields stretched back toward the ridges and along the flat area that bordered the lane—golden now in the autumn sunlight. A wordless prayer of thanks for the beauty of this land seemed to flow from her heart. She was blessed to live here, surrounded by family and dear friends on every side.

Her steps quickened as she neared the kitchen door of the farmhouse. The sound of women's voices floated out, accompanied by the smell of baking. Her mother and grandmother had already started the cookies for Grossmammi's quilting frolic the next day.

They were so engrossed in talk that they apparently didn't hear her approach. She opened the door, smiling in anticipation.

"You must not need my help with the cookies. It smells as if they're almost done."

Her mother rushed to hug her, closely followed by Grossmammi, brushing flour from her hands and transferring it to her apron. With their arms tight around her, Beth felt like a little girl again, seeking sympathy from the most important women in her life.

Wait…sympathy? She would have said she didn't need it, but she realized in an instant how much she longed to tell them everything—James's betrayal, her doubts, her fear that she was to blame for his wandering.

But she couldn't. Two people already knew, and every other person in on a secret made it more likely that something would slip. Her need to protect Benjy must be stronger than her yearning for their sympathy.

"We saved shortbread cookies to do with you," Mammi said. "We've already made the snickerdoodles and brownies."

Beth went to the sink to wash her hands. "Grossmammi, you must expect a lot of hungry women at the quilting frolic."

Her grandmother chuckled, her rosy cheeks crinkling. "Quilting is hard work. It needs a lot of fueling. Besides, everyone will be able to take some cookies home."

Obviously Grossmammi was having a good day. She hoped that would be true the next day as well, although her fellow quilters were old friends who understood.

"You can take yours today," Mammi said, handing her a bowl for the shortbread cookies. "After you do your share."

Beth set to work on the familiar recipe. Every family seemed to have its special recipe that had been handed down from generation to generation. Her family's was the rich, buttery recipe for shortbread cookies, and the thought of them made her mouth water.

Even though they'd seen each other a couple of days before, there seemed to be plenty to say. Family chatter kept them occupied until the shortbread was in the oven, when Mammi declared it was time to take a break for tea and cookies. Beth grabbed the kettle, laughingly arguing over who would fix the tea.

Grossmammi drew her to a chair. "Tell us how everything is going at the store. Do you like it? Where is Benjy today?"

"With Sarah this afternoon." She started with the last question first. "She dropped by for some apples yesterday." She paused, remembering how difficult it had been to deal with Sarah's determination to keep Benjy from doing just about everything.

"And?" Her mother had heard the unspoken thought, it seemed. "Was something wrong?"

"Not really. I was just afraid Benjy might talk back to her because she was so protective—not wanting him to climb or run or even reach for the apples."

"Did he?" Mamm asked.

"No," she admitted. "But it made me nervous the whole time. I tried to explain that those were things he normally did, but she's so cautious."

"She always was." Grossmammi took a sip of her tea. "She spoiled James with all her fussing over him, and she'll do the same with Benjy if you're not careful."

Beth glanced at her mother. Grossmammi was becoming more outspoken the older she became. What she said might be true, but Beth had to be tactful with Sarah, especially since James was gone.

"Now, Mammi," her mother said. "Beth will handle it all right. And a little fussing won't hurt the boy."

Beth held her breath, fearing an argument, but Grossmammi just shrugged. "I just don't want Benjy to be too much like his father."

Beth sought frantically for another topic of conversation. It almost sounded as if Grossmammi knew, but she couldn't.

Mammi stepped in. "How is it going at the store? Does Benjy enjoy going there or is it too much for such a little one?"

"It's definitely not too much for him." Relieved, she smiled at her mother with thankfulness. "You should see him going from one person to another trying to help. And they're all so good with him. Especially Daniel." She pictured Daniel's large hands guiding Benjy's as they worked together.

"Ach, Benjy is such a sweet boy. Of course they're gut with him." Mammi beamed with pride over her grandson.

"And Daniel is a gut man," Grossmammi added. She was still for a moment, her gaze seeming to drift to the past. "There was a time when I thought he'd be just right for our Beth." She smiled. "Maybe it's not too late, yah?"

Beth's mother drew in a shocked breath. "Mammi! It's much too early for Beth to be thinking of that."

Grossmammi chuckled. "Nothing wrong with thinking," she said, twinkling at Beth.

Shaking her head, Beth busied herself with her tea, hoping the cup would hide the fact that she might be blushing.

By the time Beth reached home, she had convinced herself that she had shown no reaction at all to her grandmother's comment about Daniel. He was a friend, and that was all.

Besides, after what had happened with James, she wasn't at all sure that she could trust anyone enough to marry again. Even if she did grow to feel more confident about her own judgment, Benjy might resent the idea of someone taking his father's place. And as her mother had said, it was much too soon to be thinking about that at all.

Benjy should be back before too long, and she suspected his grandmother would have given him several treats during the afternoon. A light supper would suit them both, and she had several quarts of the beef vegetable soup she'd made back in the spring. With only herself and a young child to feed, it had become increasingly tempting to skip making a heavy meal for supper.

She'd have time to feed the chickens before Sarah and Benjy arrived, so she headed into the mudroom to mix up the mash for the hens. But she'd barely gotten started when she heard a buggy coming up the drive.

Leaving the pail on the counter, Beth headed for the door. Sarah must be bringing Benjy back early. Maybe an active four-year-old was a bit much for her.

She stepped out onto the back porch, but the horse and buggy weren't familiar. When it drew nearer, she recognized Elijah Schmidt from the church. She knew him, of course, but he and his family were newcomers and lived on the opposite side of town, where he ran a couple of small businesses—a harness shop that

Marta Perry ·

145

his oldest son managed and a fabric store that was his wife's favorite project.

There didn't seem to be any reason for him to be calling on her, but she went forward with a welcoming smile.

"Elijah, wilkom. What can I do for you?" She stopped at the bottom of the steps. She didn't intend to ask him in. That seemed unsuitable when she was alone here.

"How are you, Beth? And your young one?" Elijah heaved his considerable bulk down from the buggy seat. He wasn't fat, she scolded herself. Just…large.

"We're fine, denke, Elijah. And your family?" She spoke the expected words, still wondering what had brought him here.

"Fine, fine." He didn't seem to be thinking of them. "I guess you're wondering what brought me here."

She was, but it didn't seem polite to say so. "Anyone of the Leit is always wilkom here. Everyone has been so kind since James's passing."

"A sad thing," he said. "In a way, you might say that's what brought me here. It's about the store."

Beth looked at him blankly. She supposed his family sometimes shopped at the store. Most of the community did, but she didn't recall seeing them.

"Your share of the store, I should say." He propped one foot on the step, the movement making him closer to her than she liked.

"I've been thinking that it must be difficult for you, having your husband's funds tied up in the business. Probably doesn't leave you and your boy much to get along with."

She stiffened, feeling the urge to say that wasn't his business. "You needn't be concerned about us. We're doing fine."

A faint look of irritation crossed his face. "You've got your family, of course, but they're busy with their own farms. So it seemed to me you might be glad of someone to buy out your share."

The comment startled her, coming out of the blue. It had always been a possibility, but she had settled in so well at the store that she hadn't thought of it at all.

"I don't think…"

He didn't let her finish. "I'd be prepared to make you a generous offer for your share of the business, cash in hand. Then you wouldn't have to worry about business at all."

The sum he named sounded like a great deal. Still, she had no idea what the store was actually worth.

She collected her thoughts. "That's generous of you, Elijah. But I don't think…"

Elijah seemed determined not to let her finish. "You'll want to talk it over with your daad, that's for sure. An inexperienced young woman like yourself wouldn't know what's fair."

Beth's impulse was to turn him down immediately, but maybe she ought to consider it. She'd been determined from the beginning that whatever she did had to be what was best for her son.

"I'm afraid I couldn't make any sudden decision. If I should want to talk about it, I'll be in touch."

Elijah's heavy eyebrows came down in a frown. "If you want. It's a fair offer. Anyone will tell you that.

And if you don't decide soon…well, I might not be interested. I'm looking to invest in another business, and I'm considering a couple of things besides the store." He leaned toward her. "I'll be glad to talk to your father anytime. An inexperienced young woman like you ought to leave the business to the men."

That was the second time he'd called her inexperienced and young, and she discovered it annoyed her. James had never said it in so many words, but she realized now that had been his attitude each time she'd suggested helping with the store.

In fact, he'd kept her in ignorance of the store's running, so that she hadn't been prepared when she had to take over his share. If not for Daniel's help…

She stopped that train of thought. She should consider Schmidt's offer carefully. But she wouldn't let anyone pressure her into a decision.

"I'll have to take that chance," she said, putting as much firmness as she could into her voice. "If I want to talk to you about it, I'll let you know."

It was more or less what she'd already said, and she wondered if he'd accept it this time. Beth could see him debating whether to push his argument or not.

At last he nodded. "Fine. I just hope I won't have to let you down."

Deciding there was nothing more to be said, Beth retreated up the steps to the porch, watching him clamber back into the buggy, turn and drive off. Her thoughts lingered on the amount of money he'd offered. It had sounded like a fortune to her, but money wasn't everything. Benjy's future was what mattered.

* * *

Daniel locked the front door of the store and stood for a moment, admiring the windows. Beth had been right about how they'd looked. Her design, with the fall colors, fall fruits and fall vegetables, made him smile when he glanced at it. Other folks had commented favorably, as well.

Did Beth know that? He didn't think he'd ever mentioned it, and he should have. Beth needed the confidence that came with doing her job well. He'd seen the look of doubt that came too often to her eyes. She still wasn't sure she was pulling her weight in the business, and he had a responsibility to see that she didn't give it up in discouragement. She had something to offer—the display proved it.

He wasn't sure why neither he nor James had ever thought about putting up a display—maybe because they'd never found it necessary to advertise. Their customers were mostly Amish who came to them because they carried the things they needed at reasonable prices. At least, he supposed that was why.

Recent years had seen an increase in Englisch customers, especially for baked goods and homemade soups. They seemed to have the feeling that those kinds of Amish goods were better. More natural, one of their customers had told him. Funny, when he thought about how the Amish teens were crazy for frozen pizza.

He stepped off the porch, feeling a little restless. Cooped up in the store all day—that was what he'd been. He ought to take a good tramp through the woods, or better yet, find out if Daad or Seth needed any help.

"Daniel!"

Before Daniel could move, a small figure came rushing toward him and grabbed him by the legs. He bent, surprised by Benjy's enthusiastic greeting, and patted his back.

"Benjy. What are you doing out here by yourself?"

Benjy was convulsed in giggles at his question. "I'm not by myself. Grossmammi is with me."

Daniel smiled at Sarah over his head. "So I see. What have you two been doing?"

"Having a busy afternoon," Sarah said, her gaze on her grandson a little perplexed.

Was she looking at Benjy and seeing his father at that age? He certainly resembled James, although the closer they became, the more he saw of Beth in her son.

"Grossmammi had apple dumplings," Benjy volunteered. "But it's time to go home now." He tugged at Daniel's hand.

Benjy sounded a little too eager for his afternoon to be at an end, and Daniel glanced at Sarah, hoping she hadn't noticed. But Sarah just looked tired, as if an active four-year-old had worn her out.

He made a sudden decision. "I have to speak to Beth about some more apples for the store. How about if I save you the walk and take Benjy the rest of the way home?"

Sarah looked relieved. "Denke." She held out her arms to Benjy. "Give me a hug now, Benjy. I'll see you soon, yah?"

Nodding, Benjy hugged her quickly before grabbing Daniel's hand again. "Denke, Grossmammi. Thank you for having me." He ran the words together, his thoughts obviously jumping ahead.

Sarah nodded, turning to walk back the way she'd come, and Benjy gave a few more hops.

"I have the wiggles," he announced. "I had to sit too much at Grossmammi's house."

"I guess you'd better run, then." He released Benjy's hand. "Go ahead. I'll be right behind."

He watched Benjy race down the lane, shaking his head a little. He'd hate to see Benjy favoring one grandparent over another, but it was only natural at his age to prefer all the things he could do on the farm. Still, Beth had a firm hand where her son's behavior was concerned.

After racing in circles a few times like a hunting dog just off the leash, Benjy trotted back to him and together they covered the rest of the distance to the house.

Benjy galloped up the steps to the porch and on into the house, letting the door bang so that it popped open again. Following him, Daniel closed the door, making sure it latched before going after him into the kitchen, where he could hear Beth's voice.

"But where is your grossmammi?" she was asking.

"I ran into them outside the store. I told Sarah I'd bring him the rest of the way." He probably shouldn't have come right into the house without asking. Things that had been normal when James was alive needed thought now.

But Beth seemed to take his presence for granted. "Poor Sarah. Was she tired out?"

"I'm afraid so." He grinned, glancing at Benjy. "Little folks are a bit much when you're not used to them."

"Were you polite, Benjamin?" She fixed him with a firm stare.

"I was," Benjy protested. "I told you I'd be gut, but there's nothing to do at Grossmammi's house."

"Well, I have something for you to do. Take out the bucket of chicken food from the mudroom. I'll have your supper ready when you get back."

Benjy rushed out, leaving Daniel alone with Beth and too aware of the fact to be comfortable.

"I'd better go so you can get your meal on." He was heading out even as he spoke.

Her light footsteps sounded as she came after him. "There was something—"

Beth grasped his arm to stop him, and as quickly as that, she seemed to forget what was in her mind. Daniel understood, because the same thing had struck him in that moment. He turned slowly, impelled by the pressure of her hand against his arm.

He'd felt it before—this compelling attraction—and fought it. But this time Beth felt it, too. He could tell by the way her lips parted and her eyes darkened.

With a wrench that seemed to tear at his heart, Daniel pulled away and hurried out.

Chapter Eleven

"Mammi, someone's coming." Benjy thundered down from the bathroom, where Beth had sent him after a look at his supposedly washed hands.

Stepping to the window, Beth saw Lydia's buggy pass the window and pull up at the hitching rail. "It's Lydia," she said, but Benjy had already raced past her, and she could hear his voice chattering away, not giving Lydia a chance to speak.

"Enough," she said, following him to the porch and putting a gentle hand on his cheek. "Let Lydia get a word in."

Grinning, Lydia gave hugs, first to Benjy and then to Beth. "Remember how excited you were when he started to talk?" she teased, making Beth smile.

"I like to talk," Benjy said. "Today I went to Grossmammi's house, and I talked to her."

"I'll bet she liked that." Lydia put an arm around his shoulders and let him lead her into the house. Beth skirted them, hurrying to stir the soup before it could stick.

"Stay for supper?" she asked with a glance at Lydia.

"Sounds gut." Lydia promptly took another plate and bowl from the cabinet, making herself at home as always. "I was hoping for soup. I had to work the supper shift because a couple of the girls were out sick. At least, they said they were sick, but I heard a rumor there was a dance over in Boonsboro tonight."

"Englisch girls, I trust," she said, amused at Lydia's accounts of her work at the diner.

"Yah, for sure."

"What's a dance?" Benjy asked.

Before Lydia could get tangled in explanations, Beth steered him toward his seat. "Climb up there, now. I'm ready to serve. No talking until after the blessing," she added, seeing him ready to repeat his question. Normally she would take the opportunity to explain the differences between the Leit and the Englisch world, but Benjy was a little young for this one, she decided.

Once the silent blessing had concluded, Benjy was too occupied spooning soup into his mouth to continue the questioning. Lydia raised her eyebrows in a question. "Which Grossmammi?"

"Sarah," she said. "I was over at my mamm's helping get ready for Grossmammi's quilting frolic."

"Your grossmammi never slows down, does she?" Lydia's smile was affectionate.

"I have three grossmammis," Benjy volunteered, obviously remembering their conversation.

Under cover of his chatter, Beth could let her mind

stray to those moments with Daniel. Awkward moments, she thought, except that it hadn't really felt awkward. Instead, it had felt familiar and comfortable.

She'd reached out to Daniel as her childhood friend, but in the instant they'd touched, he had turned into someone else entirely, and she didn't know what to do about it.

Beth was more than usually grateful for Lydia's visit. With their chatter and laughter, it had been possible to put Daniel out of her mind, at least for a short while.

After supper, she played a game with Benjy and then read to him from his favorite book. It was a relaxed evening, and gradually the stress over her reaction to Daniel subsided.

Surely it was just a momentary thing—an impulsive reaction born of loneliness and gratitude. There was nothing to worry about.

Once Benjy had gone to bed and they settled at the table, Lydia gave her a measuring look. "What's wrong? Are you fretting about that note again?"

"Note?" Her mind was blank. "Oh, no, not exactly. In fact, I burned it."

"That's *gut*, ain't so?" Lydia stirred her cup of tea absently, her gaze on Beth's face.

"I guess so." She grimaced. "I haven't forgotten it. But at least I don't think about it all the time." Especially now, when she had something new to worry her.

"I'm glad to hear it. That means you're looking ahead instead of brooding about the past."

"Sometimes I think whatever I do, I'll feel guilty.

I don't want to forget James, but when I remember what he did, I feel like he wasn't really the person I married at all."

"I can see that," Lydia said slowly. "I think so, anyway. I guess I'd feel the same."

"I hope you never have to." Since she had married James, she'd wished that Lydia might find someone to share her life with. Now…well, she didn't know.

Lydia's smooth forehead wrinkled in thought. "Did you ever think that maybe James didn't have it in him to love somebody deeply? Maybe he was just…well, all on the surface. You know what I mean," she said, growing frustrated with her inability to explain. "Some people are just deeper than others. Like your daad. Or Daniel."

The mention of Daniel jolted her back to the memory she'd been holding at bay. She tried, unsuccessfully, to shove it away again.

Could she tell Lydia? The answer came without thought. No, she couldn't. She and Lydia had shared so many things, but this…

No, she'd have to deal with this herself. She had to learn how to handle her own rebellious impulses. And if she couldn't—well, she had the answer right at hand. If she couldn't handle this, her only choice might be to sell so she could stay away from Daniel.

The following morning, Daniel was still trying to convince himself that yesterday had never really happened. Discovering he'd just dropped the onions in the bin that held sweet potatoes, he fished them back out and told himself sternly to concentrate on what he was doing.

Two minutes later, he was thinking about Beth again. Should he try to talk with Beth about it? Apologize? But she was the one who'd touched him.

His memory sent him right back to that moment—to the feel of her hand on his arm, to the sense that a current flowed between them each time they touched, to the instant that her green eyes had darkened and he'd known that she felt what he did.

Was he sure? Maybe it had been wishful thinking on his part. If she hadn't felt anything, trying to talk about it would just be embarrassing for both of them.

And even if what he thought had happened had been real, it might still be best to pretend. If they could each hold on to their composure, their partnership would be able to go on without hindrance.

Daniel's argument with himself ended abruptly when the bell on the door jingled. Looking down the row of shelves, he saw Benjy and Beth come in, with Benjy chattering away to his mother. Benjy spotted him and came running, so Daniel set the basket of onions aside and went to meet him.

"Whoa, slow down." He felt obligated to correct him about running in the store, even though it warmed his heart to see Benjy so eager.

"No running in the store," Beth reminded her son. She managed to focus on Benjy without apparently seeing Daniel, so she may have decided to ignore the incident, too.

"But I have to tell Daniel," Benjy said, grabbing

his hand. "We're going to have a cider-pressing on Saturday, and everyone is coming. Grossmammi, and grossdaadi, and my onkels and aunts and cousins and everyone. You'll come, won't you? Please?"

He looked at Beth, trying to read her reaction in her face. Would she rather he made some excuse?

"Yah, do come." She seemed to hold on to normal manner with an effort. "Everyone is coming and bringing something for supper, so we'll have a fine time. You can all take some cider home with you, like always."

Her words reminded him of other years, other cider-pressings, when he'd helped with the press while James greeted everyone. He had a moment's doubt, but probably it was right for Beth to carry on the yearly tradition. She couldn't cancel everything that was a reminder of James, and the apples would need to be processed.

He nodded. "I'll come as soon as I can get away and help with the press, if you want."

"Gut. I thought I'd ask Timothy, too. And Anna."

"Let's hurry and tell them," Benjy said. "I think they'll be happy."

He thought a sense of relief crossed Beth's face as she let her son tug her away. She probably was relieved to end her conversation with him. The less they were together, the easier it would be to let the memory of yesterday fade into nothing.

A few minutes later he heard laughter from the other side of the store, which he guessed was Benjy talking to Timothy about the cider-pressing. He'd go, for sure. Timothy was always up for anything new.

Anna he wasn't so sure about. He'd noticed Beth's

efforts to make friends with the girl, as well as Anna's lack of response. Anna could use a friend like Beth— someone young enough to remember those teen years and mature enough to steer Anna in the right direction. But with Anna's painful shyness, it would take time and patience, he thought.

The bell over the door rang, and Elijah Schmidt came in. A glance told him that no one was at the checkout counter. If Beth was talking with Anna, there was no point in interrupting them. He'd take it if Elijah showed signs of wanting to check out.

Elijah didn't move toward the register. In fact, he didn't appear to be shopping at all. He just wandered down the aisles, looking but not picking anything up. Daniel watched him, curious, for a few minutes. Then, giving in to his curiosity, he walked over to him.

"Elijah, gut to see you. Can I help you?"

Elijah gave him what seemed to be an appraising look. "Denke, but I'm not buying today. Wanted a look around, just in case."

Daniel stared at him blankly. "In case of what?"

"Didn't Beth tell you? I figured she probably told her partner everything."

Irritation made Daniel's voice sharpen. "I don't know what you mean." And he certain sure wasn't going to discuss Beth with him.

"I stopped by to see her yesterday. Been thinking about it for a time, but I didn't want to be too soon after her husband's death." He leaned against the shelf behind him, knocking over several boxes of corn bread mix. "I made an offer for James's share of the store. If it goes the way I want, I'll be your new partner. What do you think of that?"

Daniel schooled his face to express nothing of what he felt. If he'd made a list of all the people he didn't want to work with, Elijah would have been on it. Everyone knew he cut every corner that wasn't illegal in his various businesses.

He couldn't just stand here. He had to say something. "I think you'd better wait until Beth gives you an answer before you make any decision."

"We'll see." Elijah shrugged and then turned and walked off.

For a few seconds, Daniel stood with his stomach churning. Thinking about it did no good at all. He had to talk to Beth.

Just about the time he reached the storeroom, Anna hurried out. Avoiding his gaze, she murmured something about taking the checkout and skittered off.

Beth emerged from the storeroom, her troubled gaze fixed on Anna. "I don't understand Anna, I'm afraid. I thought she'd like to come to the cider-pressing. She doesn't get much fun, poor girl. But she looked terrified at the idea."

He shook his head, dismissing Anna for the moment, and gestured toward the office. "We need to talk. About Elijah Schmidt."

By the time the office door closed behind them, Beth had gone from being blindsided by Daniel's words to being annoyed at his high-handed attitude.

She didn't answer to him. She was his co-owner, not his employee.

"What's going on?"

It was practically a demand, and Beth's back stiffened. And how on earth could he know about Elijah's visit already? "What are you talking about?"

"Elijah Schmidt was here already this morning, looking around like he owned the place." Daniel's eyebrows were a dark slash across his face. "He said he's made you an offer for your share of the business."

"Did he say I'd accepted it?" she snapped. "If you'll calm down a bit, I'll tell you exactly what happened."

Daniel seemed to hear her. His chest heaved as he took a couple of deeps breaths. By the time he met her eyes again, his anger had been tempered by embarrassment.

"I'm sorry." He bit off the words and then took another breath, clearly fighting his temper. "Please tell me. Are you thinking of selling?"

Beth put up a hand, not willing to answer that question right now. "Elijah Schmidt stopped by the house yesterday afternoon. He said he wanted to talk business." She grimaced. "I think he really wanted to talk to my father, since he seemed to feel women can't possibly understand business. But that was the gist of it. He wants another business, and he's had his eye on this one. He made me an offer for my share."

"How much?" he said sharply, and then shook his head. "Sorry." He was trying not to antagonize her, she thought. "If you don't mind telling me, at least I could see if it's reasonable."

Her anger faded at Daniel's effort. The store meant the world to him. It was only natural that he'd be upset, but she couldn't let herself be influenced by that. Benjy's future was at stake with her decision. She named the amount.

Daniel considered. "It's not an awful figure, but it's worth more, in my opinion. Do you really want to sell?"

That was an impossible question. There were so many different things involved—Benjy's future, the question of a fair offer, Daniel's opinion of someone who might be his partner. And most of all, the fact that if she needed to see less of him, this was the only way of doing it.

"Not exactly." She picked her words carefully. "It would make things easier, in a way, but that's not what's important. I have to consider Benjy first."

"Wouldn't it be best for Benjy to have a successful business to step into?"

"Maybe. But he's too young to make that decision right now. I have to do it for him, and it's hard."

Her voice wavered on the last word as she thought of the weight of responsibility on her, and she could see him wince.

"Are you seriously considering it?" His voice had roughened, whether at the thought of Elijah Schmidt as his partner or at the loss of her and Benjy, she didn't know. But even if it hurt him, she had to give an honest answer.

She cleared her throat before she could say anything. She had a longing to speak openly. To say that being around him was too difficult. But that would mean admitting that she was attracted to him, and she couldn't do that.

"I have to think about it. And talk to my daad about it, despite not wanting to oblige Elijah. You understand, don't you?"

The muscles in Daniel's neck worked, but he nodded. "Yah. I understand." He hesitated. "You'd best tell your daad that he can look at the books anytime he wants."

"Denke, Daniel."

If this went on much longer, she was going to be in tears. Shaking her head, she made her way blindly toward the door. Daniel grasped the handle and opened it for her. She could feel his gaze on her as she went out, but he didn't speak. She could only be grateful.

Chapter Twelve

Daniel had suggested that Beth stay home from the store on Saturday, telling her that she had plenty to do with the cider-pressing that day. He knew that was true, but he also knew they'd been uncomfortable around each other for the last couple of days since he'd found out about the offer from Elijah.

He realized he was clenching his fists and deliberately relaxed them. He'd also been standing and staring into the meat case. He shook himself with a command to get busy and stop thinking about Beth. He could do the one but not the other.

The possibility she'd decide to sell out, combined with struggling about his feelings for her—

Again he stopped what he was doing, this time feeling as if he'd been hit in the stomach. How stupid could he be? The very fact of their attraction could be giving Beth the impetus to sell. Now that he saw it, he couldn't believe it had taken him this long.

"Onkel Daniel." Timothy sounded as if it were not

the first time he'd spoken. "Onkel Daniel, are you all right?"

"Yah, for sure." His face probably looked as if he'd seen a ghost. "What do you need?"

Instead of speaking up, Timothy stared down at his feet. "Well, I wondered… You see, I was talking to Janie, and she said she'd be at Beth's all day helping get ready for the cider-pressing." He came to a halt, and Daniel had the unique experience of seeing his self-confident nephew turning bright red.

"And?" he prompted, trying to disguise his amusement.

"Well, we're not too busy this afternoon, and I thought Janie… I mean Beth and Janie, might use my help. If I could leave early."

Daniel made a point of looking around the store, taking note of the fact that, as usual, Saturday afternoon was a slack time. In the morning they'd been busy, but not now.

"All right, you can leave now. Just make sure you're helping, not distracting…someone."

Timothy grinned, over his embarrassment. "Denke, Onkel Daniel. I'll help." With a light step, he headed for the door.

Fortunate Timothy, not wondering if it was all right to care for someone.

As for him…was there any way to relieve Beth's need to avoid him? Or was he completely wrong about the whole thing? He'd like to ease any fear she felt without offending her, and if he tried to say he didn't feel that way about her, he'd be lying.

The afternoon wore on without any answer coming to him. He'd almost rather have more work than he could handle than to have the clock crawling along at a snail's pace.

Finally it was near enough closing that he thought he could start getting ready for the closed day tomorrow. There was always a little extra to do in preparing for the Sabbath. That way he could get on his way to Beth's promptly.

Daniel walked toward the rear of the store and stopped, arrested by a noise coming from behind the shelves in the far corner. It almost sounded as if someone were crying.

Anna, he thought. It must be. He stood undecided for a moment, having the usual male reaction to coping with someone's tears. But if Anna needed help, he had a duty to give it.

Rounding the end of the shelf unit, he saw that he'd been right. Anna was crumpled into a heap on the step they used to reach the top shelf, trying to muffle her sobs with her apron.

He squatted down next to her. "I'm so sorry you're upset. Do you want to go on home? I can get the buggy out and have you there in no time."

Anna shook her head vigorously at that, choking on a sob to say she'd rather stay here. Giving a regretful thought toward the cider-pressing, Daniel sat down next to her.

"Is it your father? If you want me to talk to him…"

Another head shake, even stronger. "It's not Daadi.

But when he hears what I did…" That trailed off into a wail, and her flow of tears seemed inexhaustible.

Daniel sucked in a breath, trying to think of the comforting things his mother had said to him when everything was wrong. "Do you… Do you want to tell me about it?" He asked the question, hoping the answer was no. "If so, I promise not to tell anyone."

Her sobs lessened. "You promise?"

"Yah, for sure." What kind of trouble could a kid like Anna get into? It probably wasn't nearly as bad as she thought.

"I thought… I thought I'd die when I knew. I wish I'd died." Her voice rose, and he feared this was something way beyond his ability to cope with.

"If you'd rather talk to a woman, I could fetch Beth—"

"No, no. Not Beth. She can't know." She looked at Daniel, her face blotchy and tearstained, her eyes red. "You don't understand. It was me. I was the one James was coming to the night he died."

Daniel rocked back on his heels, nearly toppling over. Not Anna. Not a poor kid who already had more than her share of troubles. Anger soared. If he had James in front of him right now, all the faith in the world wouldn't keep him from striking out.

He forced himself to focus on Anna. "I think you'd better tell me all of it." He said the words as kindly as he could, given all the grief that had resulted from James's action.

"It wasn't…it wasn't all that bad. I mean, all we did was talk. James was so kind." Her eyes seemed to glow with the memory. "He just kissed me. Twice. That was all. He made me feel like I…like I was worth something."

"Anna, you are worth something. You're a good, kind, hardworking girl, no matter what anyone says." And James had taken advantage of that, bolstering up his ego by persuading Anna into an action that would bring her under the discipline of the church.

"I'm not. I'm wicked." The tears welled again.

Daniel had never felt quite as useless in his life. But one thing he did know. "You have to tell Beth. You know that, don't you?"

Her sobs grew shrill, probably hysterical, not that he knew what that was like. Praying no one would come into the store, he spoke softly, trying to reason with her.

It was no use. Somehow, he'd known it wouldn't be. Anna seemed incapable of facing Beth. He'd promised not to tell, so his hands were tied. How this would ever come right, he couldn't imagine.

Beth paused on the back porch to check the progress of her cider-pressing. So many people had come early to help that she couldn't believe how easily it had all come together. Daad had helped her set up the cider press, her oldest brother, Eli, had organized a team for picking the apples, and others in the family took care of washing and cutting the apples.

By now, the actual pressing had started, with everyone vying to be the one who turned the crank to crush the apples. Benjy and various cousins watched with fascination as the round metal plate was pushed down on the apples. Golden liquid began to flow into the bucket beneath the press.

Beth felt someone behind her and turned to find her grandmother.

"That's Isaac's press," she said, and Beth wondered if Grossmammi was looking at the present or the past.

"Yah, it is. He gave it to me when he sold us the property."

Grossmammi looked confused for just a second before making a mental adjustment. "It must be fifty years old. More, most likely. I remember the cider he used to make. Best in the county."

Beth nodded. "He always said it was the apples he mixed that made the difference. This year we're using a mix of Red Delicious for the sweetness and McIntosh for the tartness."

"I... I don't remember what Eli used." Her faded blue eyes clouded with confusion.

"I think he especially liked the McIntosh from that one tree. Remember? He always said they were best for cider, didn't he?"

Grossmammi's eyes cleared, and she touched Beth's cheek lightly. "Ach, I'm getting a bit forgetful. You're a gut child, putting up with my wandering."

"I'd rather listen to you wandering than most folks' babbling." She pressed her cheek against Grossmammi's, a little more withered now than it had been even a year ago. Sometimes it seemed the old got smaller and smaller and lighter and lighter until they were ready to slip right up to Heaven.

Tears stung her eyes for a moment, and she blinked

them away. Since James's death, she'd found that tears came quicker about most anything.

Grossmammi's hand closed over hers. "Just look at it." Her gaze seemed to sweep the scene, from one group of workers to another, from the golden stubble in the fields to the golden leaves carpeting the ground and the red glow of the oaks on the ridges. "It's beautiful. And it's home."

"Yah, it is." Peace flowed through Beth, wiping away for the moment the worries and indecision of her situation. They'd be waiting to spring out at her, she supposed, but she'd cling to the peace of this moment as long as she could.

Mammi came out of the kitchen and joined them. "What are you two doing?"

Beth and her grandmother exchanged a smiling glance. Grossmammi always said that Beth's mother couldn't see anyone idle without giving them a job to do, to which Mammi would answer that anyone who'd raised five children would do the same.

"Just remembering," Beth said. "Do you need some help, Mammi?"

Her mother shook her head. "Everything's ready for supper whenever you want to take a break. Just say when. Is everyone here now?"

Beth didn't need to look to see that Daniel wasn't here. Nor was Anna, though she didn't really expect Anna. She'd been firm in refusing the invitation.

But Daniel…she'd expected him to be here by now. She was ashamed to admit that she'd been watching for him. He might have been held up at the store, she supposed. And anyway, what difference did it make?

She looked down the lane for the twentieth time in the past hour. This time she spotted Daniel's sturdy figure coming toward them at an easy pace.

Her heart lifted despite her effort to tamp down her feelings. "Here comes Daniel. I think he's the last. But we'd better keep them working for now. You know how hard it is to get folks moving again after a gut meal."

When Daniel reached the group, he headed for the press, greeting the men who'd begun to gather around it. That was what she expected, she told herself. There was no need for him to greet her, after all.

Just then Timothy hauled a protesting Benjy up the steps to her. "I don't want to," he was arguing vehemently.

"Ask your mammi," Timothy said, unmoved. "If she says it's all right, then it is. But I know what happens with my little brothers if they drink that much fresh cider."

"How much?" Resigned to a bellyache, she detached her young son from Timothy's grasp.

Timothy grinned. "Six cups that I saw, but there might have been more."

"Will said he could drink ten cups of cider," Benjy said indignantly. "And I said I could drink more than he could, and he said I couldn't."

Timothy shook his head, used to dealing with his young brothers. "I'd better collect Will before Daadi hears."

"Send him into the house for some crackers," Beth

said. "Maybe that will absorb some of the cider. Denke, Timothy. I should have been watching for that."

With a firm hand she guided her son into the kitchen. "Didn't I tell you not to drink more than two cups?"

"But it was gut…" Benjy said, but he stopped, apparently realizing that his mother wouldn't be moved.

In a few minutes Beth had her son and young Will at the table with some crackers in front of them. "There," she said. "Eat all of those, even if you don't want it. I told you not to drink more because too much fresh cider will make your tummy hurt."

Her mother, who'd come in with them, sliced off a couple of pieces from the loaf on the counter and added them to the boys' plates. "Bread will help, too. You want to be able to eat some of that fried chicken I brought, don't you?"

Both of the boys nodded vigorously and applied themselves to eating. Mammi chuckled and glanced at Beth. "You go on and do what you need to do. I'll keep track of these two."

Hoping Timothy had caught the boys in time, Beth went out, wondering why little boys got twice as many bad ideas when they were together as when they were alone.

No sooner had she reached the bottom of the stairs than she found Daniel blocking her way. He hastily stepped back. "Sorry. I was just coming to look for you. Your daad wants to know if there are any more jugs for the cider. Looks like he'll need about two more to finish up this pressing."

There was no reason for her to feel awkward around

Daniel, she reminded herself. He was the one who'd been unreasonable about Elijah Schmidt.

"I washed them all and put them in the pantry." Gesturing him to follow her, she went back inside. "I'll show you."

She led him into the shelf-lined pantry, filled with canned foods. One section of shelves she used for canning jars and other containers, and on the floor she'd set the extra jugs. "Here you are." She hesitated. "I'm glad you came. I was afraid…"

Daniel had bent to grasp the glass containers, but he straightened at that, the movement bringing him close to her. "I was delayed, or I'd have been here earlier. I wanted to say how sorry I am for the way I acted about Elijah Schmidt. I jumped to conclusions."

Beth glanced down, not sure she wanted to meet his steady gaze. "It wasn't your fault. I did intend to tell you about the offer. I just…well, I was trying to find the right way to do it."

Neither of them said anything for a moment. Was he hoping she'd say she'd already refused the offer? She couldn't do that, not when she didn't know her own mind.

Apparently deciding she wasn't going to say any more, Daniel bent and picked up two of the jugs. "It's all right," he said, his voice colorless, and walked out with the jugs.

Beth stood looking after him, frustrated with him and with herself. It was all very well to resolve to move forward, but how could she when her emotions were such a tangled mess?

* * *

Worship was at her friend Esther's house on Sunday, so once Beth had turned her horse and buggy over to one of the boys taking care of them, she sent Benjy to join his grandparents and headed for the kitchen to see if she could help.

Esther, looking rather frazzled, was directing a kitchen crew consisting of her sisters along with the twins Ella and Della. Lydia must have come in just ahead of her, because she was already asking if she could help.

"I'll help, as well," Beth said, bumping her elbow against Lydia's.

She grinned and added, "Yah, both of us."

Esther looked at the clock and then at the workstations in her kitchen much as Beth had surveyed the cider-making crews the previous day. "Denke, but I think we're all right now. If you'll help with serving or cleanup…"

"Right, we'll be here," Lydia said, after a glance at Beth for her approval. She caught hold of Beth's arm as they went out, stopping her when they were far enough from the various groups not to be heard.

"What's wrong?" Her grasp tightened.

Beth, taken by surprise, could only stare. "Does it show?"

"Probably not to everyone," Lydia said. "But you ought to know you can't hide things from me."

Beth glanced around to ensure that no one was nearby. Even so, she wouldn't discuss her confused feelings over Daniel, not here. "Elijah Schmidt stopped by the house a couple days ago. He offered to buy my share of the store."

Lydia's eyebrows shot up. "That's a shock. I wouldn't have thought he had ambitions to be a grocer."

Beth hadn't thought of that, but now that Lydia had mentioned it, she realized that it surprised her, as well. "I don't know that he does," she said slowly. "But he does seem…well, proud…of his businesses. And he offered me what seemed like quite a lot for it."

"Are you going to accept?" Lydia seemed to be keeping her face deliberately blank.

"You don't need to worry. I'm not asking you to tell me what to do. I'd just like to talk it over." And something even more troubling to her peace of mind. "Can you come over after work? Maybe tomorrow?" Seeing her mother looking at her, she began moving.

"Definitely tomorrow," Lydia said. "We'd best get in line, or your mother is going to blame me for detaining you. She always did think I talked too much. And she was probably right."

Smiling, Beth squeezed her hand, relieved at just the thought of talking this over with a good friend. Lydia was the only one who knew enough to give her an unbiased opinion.

When she reached her family, Daad gave her a frowning look.

"They're not ready to go in yet," she pointed out, feeling as guilty as she would have in similar circumstances when she was a child. In some things, her parents didn't think she'd grown up.

"Just don't want you to be late." He didn't smile, but

his eyes began to twinkle. "Your mamm and I remember how you girls always did talk."

"That's what friends are for," she said. "Where is Benjy?"

"With your brother. He and Will want to sit together."

Beth raised her eyebrows. "I hope he realizes what he's in for. Those two boys together are five times as mischievous as they are one at a time."

"They're a pair of snickelfritzes, all right," Daad said indulgently. "But Eli can handle them."

Things were changing, Beth realized as she hurried to her place in the line. Not that long ago, Benjy had clung to her at the very suggestion of sitting apart from her. Now he'd trotted off without even asking her. Her little boy was growing up.

Before she could decide how that made her feel, the line began to move, and they were entering the pole barn for worship. Even as she sat down and the unmarried girls filed into the benches in front of her, she realized that Anna was missing. A quick glance showed her that the rest of the family was there. She hoped Anna wasn't sick, both for her sake and because it was sometimes difficult to get along without her.

At the end of the three-hour service, she and Lydia scurried out to join the women who were serving. But Daad must have left quickly as well, because he caught up with her before she could reach the kitchen.

"A word with you," he said. At his look, Lydia moved away.

"I'll get started," she said. "Don't hurry."

"What's wrong, Daad?" His expression told her this was more serious than being late to get into line.

"There's talk going around," he said bluntly. "Talk that Elijah Schmidt is buying your share of the store."

Beth saw red. "That man—I'd like to tell him just what I think. But not on the Sabbath," she added. Hurriedly.

"So it's not true?" Daad touched her arm and leaned a little closer, as if hinting that she shouldn't lose control.

"It's true he made an offer to buy my share." She tried to arrange her thoughts. "It was that day I'd been baking with Mammi and Grossmammi. He stopped by when I got home. I certain sure didn't say that I would. I haven't even decided if I want to sell."

Her father's face seemed to relax. "I thought you wouldn't do that without telling us."

"I certain sure wouldn't," she said, a little indignant. "I want to have a talk with you about it. Soon. I want to do what's best for Benjy."

"It's not right for Elijah to go around acting as if you'd decided." Daad frowned. "I don't understand why he'd do that."

She thought she did, and she didn't like it. "I think he's trying to push me into selling."

"Then he's being foolish," Daad said. "No one can do that."

She was surprised at the implied compliment. "That doesn't mean I don't want your opinion."

"I'll look into it for you, if you want," he said. "But your mamm and I know the decision has to be yours."

He patted her hand. "You're recovering now. Getting more like yourself after the shock. We trust you to make the right choices."

"Really?" She raised her eyebrows questioningly.

He chuckled. "If I tried to tell you what to do, you'd think I was interfering, ain't so?"

Beth squeezed his arm. "You are a very gut father. Do you know that?"

"I had gut material to work with," he replied.

"Denke, Daadi." Her heart warmed.

"One thing," Daad said, cautioning. "You'll talk to Daniel about it, ain't so? After all, he and James built that business together."

She nodded, hearing the truth of his words. The little they'd spoken about it could hardly be called an actual conversation. She had to do that, no matter how uncomfortable it was.

Chapter Thirteen

❧

Daniel finished his lunch in a hurry and made his way to the other side of the barn, where he hoped to find some peace. Everyone was talking about Elijah Schmidt buying Beth's share of the store as if it was a done deal.

What if it was? Or would be? This was an eventuality he and James had never considered when they'd made up the simple agreement between them. Maybe they should have.

Well, they hadn't, so he and Beth would have to figure it out. He wanted what was best for her and Benjy, but they might have different opinions as to what that best was.

"Daniel?"

He swung around at the sound of the voice he'd recognize anywhere. Beth stood a few feet away from him.

A quick glance told him no one else was in sight, though he could hear the hum of voices from the other side of the barn.

"How did you find me?" He felt as if he'd been thinking of her so much it was like sending out signals to her. But that was just silly.

"What did you always do when you were upset?" She moved a bit closer, resting her hand on the fence railing. "Run away and hide, that's what. Since your buggy was still there, I knew you hadn't gone home, so I just looked for a likely hiding place."

"I could have been in the barn loft," he said lightly, trying to hide the stress of Elijah's offer.

She just shook her head, looking out across the field toward the road that would soon be filled with buggies. He could lean back against the fence and study her without being seen.

Beth looked different this morning, and he tried to figure out how. And why. Ever since James's death she'd been a shadow of herself, worn out by trying to cope with his death as well as the knowledge of his betrayal.

Now she'd become more definite—likc watching the fog lift from the valley, allowing the colors to come out again. Beth was finding her way back to herself, and he was thankful.

"Elijah has been talking again," she said. "I told Daad the only reason I could see is that he hopes to push me into agreeing."

"Is it working?" he asked, trying not to let his feelings show.

"It's more likely to have the opposite effect." Her voice was tart in a way he hadn't heard for a time. "I have to keep reminding myself that I should consider what's best for everyone, especially Benjy. His future is the most important thing."

He couldn't argue with that, even if he wanted to.

"Daad reminded me that we haven't actually talked it over yet—you and I, I mean."

"My fault," he said, knowing it was true. "I over-reacted. I'm—"

"You already said you're sorry," Beth said. "It's all right. Now tell me what you really think about it."

Daniel frowned, staring down at his hands grasping the top rail of the fence. "I can't really be fair, I think. James always talked about how Benjy would come into the business with us as he grew. I got so used to thinking that way that I can't picture anything else."

"Yah, I know." Beth's voice was soft, remembering. "One day that could happen, but in the meantime… well, I worry that I can't pull my own weight when it comes to running the store."

"Don't think that," he said quickly. He could hardly tell her that he lived in anticipation of the next time she was in the store. "You're doing a fine job. Nobody expects you to replace James, but you have your own things that you do well. We're doing all right the way we are."

"Denke, Daniel. But even if that's so, and you're not just trying to make me feel useful, I have to con-sider other things."

"Like the money you'd get from selling," he fin-ished for her. "It seems like a lot, but money runs out eventually. And then Benjy wouldn't have a business to inherit."

"That's true, but it's not what I was thinking about."

He looked at her, surprised by the remark, to find her smiling at him.

"What I wanted to know was how it would work out for you, having Elijah as your partner."

"Elijah." He let out a long breath, trying to think what he should say. Truthfully, he hated the idea of working with the man, but he didn't want to put Beth on the spot.

Before he found the right words, she added, "What you really think, please. What you would say if he weren't part of the church family."

He was surprised into a smile. "That makes it even harder, yah? I can't say I'd enjoy having him as a partner. James and I always had the same picture of what the store was going to be—that we'd give value to our customers and deal with them fairly and kindly. Like delivering things without charge to those folks who can't get out."

"You don't think Elijah would go along with that vision?"

He hated to speak negatively of a member of the Leit, but he couldn't be less than honest with Beth. "Based on how he runs the businesses he has, no."

"Neither do I," she said. "So that weighs against selling." She paused, seeming to consider her decision. "If it were just my concern, I'd turn him down, but I have to remember that it's Benjy's future."

He nodded. That was only right. "Take your time. Talk to anyone you want. I'm not in any hurry. Whatever you decide, I won't argue."

"Denke." Relief flooded her face. "I don't want to be at odds with you. No more misunderstandings between us—it's much better to speak honestly, yah?"

He immediately thought of his promise—of the thing he should tell her but couldn't. No. He corrected himself even as he had the thought. It wasn't he who should tell Beth. It was Anna. That poor girl would never be whole until she'd confessed to the person she'd hurt.

Beth seemed to take his agreement for granted, so he didn't have to speak.

An image of the life he really wanted arose in his mind—a picture of himself and Beth together, with Benjy growing up and working beside him. It seemed very far away.

Church Sundays usually meant having supper with family, but Beth had begged off for once. After having been occupied with the cider-making the previous day, she was more than ready for a little quiet, and she thought Benjy could use some downtime, too. Even his boundless energy should get a rest once in a while.

"How about this one, Mammi?" Benjy, helping her pick some vegetables in the garden for supper, parted the leaves of a butternut squash plant to show one. "Should I pick it?"

She stepped over a row of fading tomato plants to look closer. "I think it needs to get a bit bigger," she said, knowing that Benjy liked picking better than any other part of gardening. "See if you can find a pepper ready, and we'll have it in salad."

Benjy grimaced, salad was not his favorite dish, but he went obediently to the pepper plants.

Beth stared absently at the tomato plants, thinking about everything that had happened that morning. Daad, despite his determination not to make decisions for her, had agreed to look into the offer for her. He would be fair, and he'd be able to find out more about Elijah's reputation as a businessman than she would.

Most men would have jumped at the chance to have a full-time partner instead of an inexperienced woman with a child only able to work part-time. But Daniel clearly didn't want to work with Elijah, although his determination to do the best for his old friend's family would govern his reactions. If she decided to accept Elijah's offer, he'd deal with it.

She was fortunate to have a friend like Daniel. She firmly kept her thoughts away from any suggestion that he might, one day, be more than a friend.

Movement caught her eye, and Beth realized that a buggy was coming down the lane. To her surprise, it was Sarah, James's mother.

"Benjy, look who's coming."

"Grossmammi!" Benjy shouted, jumping over several rows and knocking down the remains of one tomato plant in his rush to greet a visitor.

By the time Beth reached them, Benjy had helped tie up the buggy horse and hugged his grandmother. Beth was just in time to hear what he said.

"Did you bring me a treat?"

"Benjy!" Aghast, Beth didn't know what to say.

"Never, never, ask someone for a treat. That is very rude."

Benjy's eyes filled with tears at the sharpness in her tone. She longed to apologize, knowing her reaction was at least partly because it was her mother-in-law. But she couldn't do that. Benjy had to learn what was acceptable and what wasn't.

She bent over him, intent on explaining. "Sometimes people bring you a little present and sometimes they don't, but we should never expect it. Then it's a nice surprise when it happens. Understand?"

He blinked away the tears and nodded. "Yah, Mammi. I'm sorry, Grossmammi."

Beth wasn't sure what Sarah would say, but she just smiled and nodded.

Relieved, Beth straightened. "We're so glad to see you. Will you stay for supper with us?"

Sarah hesitated. "Not if it's inconvenient. I just thought I'd like to talk a bit."

Beth caught the sideways flicker of her eyes toward Benjy and realized she meant in private.

"For sure. We were just getting some vegetables for supper. Benjy, will you bring one of the small baskets and pick a few things for Grossmammi to take home?"

He nodded vigorously and dashed off to the shed for a basket.

"I'm sorry," Beth began, not sure how to apologize for correcting Benjy in front of her.

But Sarah spoke at the same time. "I'm sorry," she said. "I'm afraid I've given Benjy too many treats. I know that's not good for him."

She hadn't expected an admission from her mother-in-law, and she didn't know how to handle it. "Well, I... I've noticed he doesn't eat his meals properly if he's had too many treats." She'd have called it junk food, but that would probably insult Sarah, who always had a stash of candy bars in her pantry.

"You're right, I know. It's a bad habit of mine." Sarah paused for a moment, apparently thinking of something she wanted to say. "I was thinking..."

"What is it, Sarah?" Beth gestured toward the back porch. "Let's sit down and talk."

Sarah nodded, following her to the porch swing, where they settled to watch Benjy searching through the garden with his basket.

Sarah cleared her throat. "It was so nice of you to let me have Benjy every Wednesday afternoon." She sounded so reluctant that Beth couldn't guess what was coming.

"But I was thinking that there's not much for an active little boy to do at my house."

Beth had the horrified idea that he'd broken something his grandmother valued. "If he broke something—"

"No, no." Sarah actually smiled. "He's fine. I just wanted to say that maybe he'd enjoy it more if I came over here instead of having him come to my place. My friend Alice was saying...you know Alice King...that lively little boys need to be outside playing or helping, not sitting in the house coloring pictures." She smiled ruefully. "Alice has twelve grandchildren, so she knows."

Beth nodded, relaxing. She'd half expected there was a criticism coming, but it seemed not.

"I think that would be very nice. And I could work in the afternoon or do my shopping without worrying about Benjy."

Sarah relaxed, as well. "That's gut. I want to be helpful." She watched Benjy, choosing a tomato for her. "I've been thinking so much about…about James."

Her voice shook a little, and Beth clasped her hand.

"I'm afraid I spoiled James a bit when he was little. Being the only one. But I don't want to make the same mistake with Benjy."

It was almost as if she were apologizing to Beth about James, and she wasn't quite sure what to say.

Finally, when the silence grew too long, she patted Sarah's hand. "Denke, Sarah. We'll work together on that, yah?"

Sarah smiled. "We will."

"Maybe sometimes Alice could come over with you and bring one of her grandchildren. It would be nice for Benjy to have someone to play with."

"Yah, that's a gut idea," Sarah said. "It's not right for Benjy to be an only child." She stopped for a breath. "I just wanted you to know that if the time comes that you want to marry again, I'd be happy for you."

That took Beth's breath away. She wouldn't have expected that from Sarah, and she couldn't help but wonder if Sarah might have heard rumors about James's flirting.

She chose her words carefully. "I don't see that happening anytime soon, but even if it should, you would always be Benjy's grossmammi."

Maybe it was good that Benjy came hurrying toward them, the basket bouncing against his legs. Anything else said between them would probably result in tears.

She patted Sarah's hand and stood up to rescue the basket. "Denke," she said softly, meaning it with all her heart. Sarah had just given her a gift, and she wouldn't forget it.

Beth arrived at the store ready to work Monday morning, leaving Benjy with her niece Janie. It was a sunny, brisk morning, and she'd heard them planning to rake leaves. In her experience, jumping in the piles they made would probably leave the yard looking about the same as it had been, but it would keep them busy and happy.

To her surprise, Timothy was running the checkout, something he didn't usually do. She spotted Daniel back at the meat counter helping a customer, but there was no sign of Anna.

Removing her sweater, she hurried to the counter. "Do you need me to take over for you? Where's Anna?"

He shook his head and shrugged his shoulders at the same time. "I don't know. She just didn't show up this morning, so Onkel Daniel trusted me with the checkout." He grinned, obviously pleased at what he probably thought was a promotion.

"I'll go and see where he wants me to work."

Timothy's customer asked him something just then, so not waiting for an answer, she went back to where

Daniel was wrapping a chuck roast for one of the Stoltzfus cousins. Emma smiled, asked her how she was, and then took her package and went off without waiting for an answer. Used to her ways, Beth just smiled and looked at Daniel.

"I understand we're shorthanded today. Have you heard anything about Anna?"

Stripping off the gloves he'd worn to cut the beef, Daniel shook his head. "Not a word from her. No one has called, but then Hiram probably wouldn't."

"No, I suppose not." Anna's father was extremely conservative and boasted that he'd never used a telephone. "She wasn't at worship yesterday."

"Maybe she's sick." Daniel looked more concerned than she'd have expected. "I'd think they could have sent a message."

"I should have asked her mother about it after worship, but I was busy." She'd been busy talking to him, in fact. She'd thought they'd cleared the air between them, but Daniel seemed restrained this morning.

After the way Elijah had behaved, talking as if a deal was settled between them, she felt a strong urge to tell Daniel that she had no intention of selling out to Elijah. Despite the difficulties that had arisen between her and Daniel, she really wanted to keep things exactly as they were.

She almost spoke, but she was deterred by the fact that she'd asked Daad to look into Elijah's offer. She shouldn't decide without listening to him.

Daniel still seemed withdrawn, or maybe he was just

worrying about Anna and how to run the store short-handed on what was usually a busy day.

"What do you want me to do?"

Daniel was quiet for a moment, his forehead knotted in thought. Or worry. Finally he looked at her.

"If you don't mind, I'd like it if you could go over to the Fishers' place and check on Anna."

"Go there," she repeated. "But don't you need me here? I'm sure we'd have heard if there were something seriously wrong with Anna."

"We can handle things here." His face set stubbornly. "I'd go myself, but a woman is much more likely to get answers."

In the face of his obvious concern, there was nothing she could do but agree.

"All right. I'll go this afternoon if Janie can stay with Benjy."

Daniel was already shaking his head. "Look, I can't explain, but I think something's wrong. Anna…" He stopped, and then he started again. "She hasn't been herself recently. You're the right person to do it, Beth."

There was an odd but compelling emphasis in his voice that Beth found contagious. Anna had been odd—almost in tears when Beth invited her to the cider-pressing.

"All right. I'll go back to the house and get the mare harnessed. I'll be back as soon as I can."

Now that she'd decided, Beth found she was hurrying down the lane. Common sense told her that this was an unnecessary trip, but the more she thought about Anna's behavior, the odder it was.

Benjy came running when he saw her. "Mammi, are you going to help us rake leaves?"

She looked over his head to Janie and shook her head. "I'm afraid not. I have to get Daisy harnessed up and do an errand. You do a gut job with Janie, yah?"

He pouted a bit, but before he could say anything, Janie had caught his hands and swung him around. "Let's see who makes the biggest pile of leaves."

Beth hurried on to the small barn. It was a matter of minutes to hitch Daisy to the small buggy, and she was on her way. She'd picked up the sense of urgency from Daniel, so she let Daisy trot out quickly. The mare was eager to move on such a brisk morning, so they were through town and on their way to the Fisher farm without problems.

Once Beth had left town behind, she started wondering what kind of reception she'd get. Daniel had been right in saying that she'd have a better chance at getting in than he. Etta Fisher knew her fairly well, although they weren't close friends. Etta's husband didn't seem to encourage her to share in the quiltings and work frolics that the other women did.

All she could do, it seemed to her, was to be honest. She was concerned because Anna didn't come to work today and had missed worship. If there was anything she could do...

As she turned into the lane to the Fisher place, she pulled up Daisy to focus on a prayer that her words would be guided and that she'd be able to help Anna. She'd like to pray that Hiram wouldn't be home, but that didn't seem quite right.

She drew up at the hitching rail outside the run-down farmhouse. Hiram must feel it would be prideful to paint his house and outbuildings. Climbing down, she took a deep breath and knocked on the door. Nothing showed at any of the windows, and for a moment she thought no one was home.

Then she heard slow footsteps coming to the door. It swung open. Etta stared at her for a moment.

Summoning up her courage, she said, "I've come to see Anna. We were worried when she didn't come—"

Etta interrupted her by seizing her by the arm and pulling her in. She looked down the road and then shut the door. "Hiram is at the sawmill." She said the words as if it explained her actions.

Beth tried to focus. "Is Anna all right? I should have asked you about her when I saw she wasn't in church."

Etta shook her head. "She wouldn't go. She won't do anything. She just sits in her room and cries."

"I… I'm so sorry. If there's anything I can do, I'm happy to." What could be wrong with the child? A few dark possibilities crept into her mind and were chased out again.

"Denke, Beth." Etta clutched her arm. "Maybe she'll come out for you." Her face worked as she tried to control herself. "I'm at my wit's end."

Fearing she wasn't up to this mission, Beth followed Anna's mother up the dark stairs to the upper hall that was equally dark. Etta gestured toward a door.

"That's Anna's room. If you can get her to talk…" Her eyes filled with tears. "Please, Beth. Please try."

Chapter Fourteen

Taking a deep breath, Beth tapped at the door. "Anna? It's Beth. May I come in?"

A muffled sob was the only answer.

Etta reached around her to turn the knob. The door swung open and Etta practically pushed her into the room.

Anna was curled up in a ball on the bed. She glanced up and then promptly hid her face.

But that look was enough for Beth. Anna's face was pale and drawn, as if she hadn't been eating, and her skin was blotchy from crying. Red-rimmed eyes had glanced briefly at Beth before Anna clamped them shut as if she couldn't bear to see.

Beth's heart cramped at the sight. The poor girl— whatever had happened, she desperately needed to have someone on her side. She probably wasn't the answer Anna needed, but she had to try.

Sinking down on the bed next to Anna, Beth put her arms around the girl, ignoring Anna's wince into herself. "Hush now, Anna. It's going to be all right. You don't need to worry. I'm here."

They were the simple phrases she used with Benjy—probably the very ones her mother had used with her. They might not make a lot of sense, especially since she didn't know what was wrong, but they soothed. So often in recent months she'd longed to feel someone's arms around her and to hear someone whisper that it was all right.

She kept on patting Anna's back, repeating the soothing words over and over. Gradually the hysterical weeping lessened. Beth wrapped her arms more closely around her. "It's all right. Just tell me what's happened."

Another strangled sob sounded. "I'm sorry," Anna whispered, seeming unable to make any louder noise. "I'm sorry, Beth. I'm so sorry."

Beth began to be exasperated. If Anna couldn't tell her anything, how could she help her?

"Komm now, Anna. Tell me what's wrong. Can you sit up here beside me and talk?"

Anna nodded, so Beth helped her to sit up. There, that was a step in the right direction.

"That's better. It's going to be all right. Just tell me what's wrong."

Anna tried to speak, but her voice broke on a sob. "I never wanted you to know. I never wanted anyone to know. He said no one would ever know."

He. The word set up a faint train of thought, misty and unclear, but frightening.

"Everyone will hate me." Anna's voice was stronger.

Beth sensed it would all come out now, and fear gripped her. It wasn't too late. She could run away, pretend she didn't know...

But she couldn't. There was no sense in hiding from the truth.

"It was you, wasn't it? You were the one who wrote to James." The words weren't an accusation. They were a statement of fact.

"You know?" Anna raised horrified eyes to her. "How did you know? He said no one would ever know."

Oh, James, how could you? Anna is a sixteen-year-old child. What were you thinking?

But she knew the answer to that, didn't she? He hadn't been thinking. He'd been scattering his careless charm over anyone female, and this time it had exploded in his face.

"I found a note in James's drawer. It was probably the last one you wrote—about meeting you in the usual place." She ought to feel rage, but instead all she felt was grief, both for Anna and for herself. "What was the usual place?"

Anna mopped her eyes, but she avoided looking at Beth. "That...that old schoolhouse. Down on Owl Hollow Road. We...we thought no one would see us there. But that night he didn't come, and I had to go home." A sob interrupted her. "The next day I heard..."

Anna didn't want to finish that thought, and neither did Beth.

Another sob burst from Anna. "I was just so unhappy. And when he smiled at me, it made me feel better."

"So you started meeting in secret." She couldn't help the edge to her words.

"You don't think—" Anna's eyes opened wide. "It was never anything. Just talking, and sometimes he gave me a hug. He kissed me two times." She put her hand on her cheek, as if cherishing it. "But it was wrong, and now you'll hate me. Everyone will know, and I'll be under the bann, and Daadi will be so angry…"

"Hush, hush a minute." Everyone would know. Anna would be hurt, but she wasn't the only one.

Everyone would talk, and she'd know they were talking about her, pitying her. Sarah would find out about the son she adored. How could she even survive that? And worst of all, Benjy would know. He wouldn't understand, not now, but he'd be aware that his daadi had done something shameful. Someday he'd understand, and that would be even worse.

In all her initial need to know who the woman was, she'd never considered how that would come about and what damage it would do. If only she could see another way…

She studied Anna, who had lapsed back into misery again. Anna would never be able to keep quiet about it. She had confessed because she couldn't go on, and her conscience would force her to complete the act and confess to the church.

Beth rubbed her forehead, feeling a band tighten around it as she tried to see a way out. Maybe…maybe there was a way to do the least harm possible.

"Anna, listen to me. Can you keep quiet about this a little longer now that you've told me?"

"But I have to confess, and then the whole church will know. And Daadi will be so angry…"

For an instant she wanted to shake the girl and shake Hiram Fisher, as well.

"I know. Just another day, to give me time to think this out. That's not too much, is it?"

She couldn't see any hope in Anna's face, but at least she didn't look quite so miserable.

"I'll try, if you say so."

"Gut." She didn't have a plan, and she certain sure hadn't dealt with her own feelings, but she saw a glimmer of hope. "Now, listen. I want to tell your mother that you're feeling better, and you're going to come to work tomorrow, all right?"

Anna seemed to shrink. "How could I? Everyone would be looking at me."

"You can work in the storeroom, if you want. Just do this for me, and I'll try to help you. All right?"

She sniffled a little, but then she nodded. "Denke, Beth. Daniel said I should tell you the truth, and he was right. I'll do whatever you say."

Daniel. So Daniel had known, and he hadn't told her.

Beth pushed that into the back of her mind to be dealt with later. She had enough to handle right now.

"Now you go and wash your face and freshen up. I'm going to talk to your mother, but I'll see you tomorrow at the store." She hesitated, fearing Anna would slump back into despair the instant she was gone. "Anna, I forgive you. And I'm sure God forgives you. It's going to be all right."

"I don't… I don't deserve that."

"Never mind that. Just do as I say. It will be all right."

She hoped. At the moment all she wanted was to be alone so that she could think all of this out. The important thing now was to handle it in a way that would hurt as few people as possible. She would deal with her own pain later.

The day seemed to drag by after Beth left, despite how busy they were. Daniel longed for Beth's return and dreaded it at the same time.

If she succeeded in seeing Anna, she probably knew the truth about Anna and James by now. And she'd also know that Anna had told him and that he'd kept silent.

It had been the right thing to do, hadn't it? It was far better for Anna to confess to the person she'd wronged. Beth would be more likely to believe and forgive if she heard it from Anna.

Where did that leave him? Beth, with her tender heart, would most likely forgive Anna, but it was less likely that she'd forgive him. He might very well have lost her forever.

The Monday morning press of customers had eased off abruptly, and the store was silent except for Timothy dragging a carton across the floor. Daniel planted his hands on the counter and leaned on them, head down, pain dragging at him. He didn't see a good outcome from this for anyone, and he feared he'd be a good long while forgiving James for leaving such a mess to be cleaned up.

Daniel jerked out of his painful thoughts at the

sound of footsteps behind him. Beth had come in the back door, and a glance through the side window told him that her horse and buggy were parked at the hitching rail.

He forced himself to meet her eyes, afraid of what he'd see there. He didn't find the anger he'd expected, not now at least. Beth seemed distracted, as if she were trying to figure something out.

Unable to stand the silence, he spoke. "Were you able to see her?"

Beth focused on him. "I saw her. She was shut up in her room weeping, but I finally got her talking. So far her parents don't know anything, and I convinced her not to say anything about it until I'd had a chance to decide how to handle this."

"Do you think you can rely on that?" Anna didn't strike him as someone who'd be able to keep a secret. Still, she'd done it this long.

"I don't know." She rubbed her forehead, her face pale against the black brim of the bonnet she'd worn for the drive. "I hope so. I told Etta that it was a misunderstanding. That she'd made a mistake, and she thought we were blaming her, but we're not."

She caught his look, and her eyes snapped. "I didn't lie," she said. "With that father of hers, it will be better if this isn't generally known."

Daniel frowned, feeling his head begin to hurt just as much as hers probably did. "I don't see how you're going to manage that. Anna won't be able to forgive herself until she's made it right, and that means confessing."

Beth's anger seemed to spark. "And what will happen if she confesses before the church? Everyone will know, and a lot of people will be hurt. Think of Sarah, learning that about her son. She's already at the point that she'll never stop grieving. I can't do that to her. And think of Benjy."

"And you." Daniel added the words in a soft voice. "Do you think I don't realize that? You'll be hurt twice over by what James did."

Should he have laid the blame so firmly on James? He couldn't help believing that James was the most culpable. He was a grown man, and Anna was just an impressionable child, longing to idolize anyone who was kind to her.

Beth seemed to shrug that off. "I'm wondering what would happen if I went to see the bishop with Anna. After all, they didn't...commit adultery." She struggled with the word, and he saw her wince with pain. "Maybe he'd agree to a private confession and penalty."

He considered. What she said was true, in a way. This wouldn't, he thought, rise to the level of a kneeling confession in front of the whole Leit. With the bishop's agreement, she might be able to minimize the backlash hurting innocent people.

"Can you really do that, Beth? Can you go to the bishop and listen to the story all over again?"

She shrugged. "It's the least I can do, don't you think? She's hardly more than a child. James...well, James should have known better."

That was putting it mildly, he thought. "Do you want me to go with you and Anna?"

Her anger flashed again. "Why would you do that? Because Anna confessed to you, and you didn't tell me?"

He met her eyes steadily. "You're angry with me."

"Don't I have a reason? You could have told me this. I trusted you."

"Yah, I could have told you. But I thought it would be better for Anna if she confessed to you herself. That's why I pushed you into going over there today."

He saw her absorb his reasoning, but he didn't see any indication that she agreed with it.

After a moment, Beth shook her head irritably. "Anna is coming in to work tomorrow. I thought she should be out of the house. I'll try to talk to Bishop Thomas before that to find out when he can see us."

He nodded. There didn't seem to be any answer to make. Beth was facing a painful situation, and she wouldn't let him help her. He'd forfeited that right.

There was no hope left for them, but that didn't change his feelings. He would love her forever.

Beth went home, feeling as if she'd like to get into bed and sleep for the next twenty-four hours. It couldn't be done. She had a son to take care of, and she must contact the bishop and set up a time to see him tomorrow.

That was easier said than done. She'd have to call and leave a message on the bishop's answering machine and hope he'd check it sometime soon. And she'd have to put enough urgency into her voice so that he'd see them tomorrow. She didn't think Anna could contain herself any longer than that.

As she neared the house, Benjy came running toward her. "Mammi, Mammi! You should see the big pile of leaves we made."

Beth hugged him, holding him close a bit longer than usual and inhaling the sweet little boy scent. When he wiggled to be free, she let him go reluctantly.

"Show me your leaf pile."

He looked confused for a minute, glancing around as if he thought to see it right next to him.

Janie giggled, and he started to giggle, too.

"We jumped in it too many times, didn't we, Benjy?" Janie caught his hand and swung it back and forth. "But it was lots and lots of fun."

"Yah, it was." He seemed satisfied. "We could make another one."

Beth touched his cheek lightly. "I have to make a phone call first. And maybe we should get something to eat."

"Grossdaadi is going to pick me up," Janie said. "He wanted me to tell you that he'd like to talk to you for a few minutes."

She nodded. He must have looked into the possibility of selling. She'd about decided to forget it, but she'd been so tied up today that she'd have to rethink the whole question.

Benjy tugged on Janie's hand. "Doesn't Grossdaadi want to talk to me?"

"I'm sure he does," she said, smiling. "Let's go fix a snack while Mammi is making her phone call."

In a few minutes, Beth was walking back from the phone shanty. If she'd sounded as desperate as she felt,

Bishop Thomas would probably want to see her immediately.

When she got in the house, she realized it was well past lunchtime and she hadn't even noticed it. Janie caught her dismayed look at the clock and shook her head, smiling.

"It's all right. Benjy and I had our lunch already. We'll have some cider and cookies now. Can I fix something for you?"

"I'm not hungry," she said quickly, afraid she wouldn't succeed if she tried to eat something now. "I'll wait and see if your grandfather wants something."

Janie seemed to be studying her, catching on to the fact that she wasn't as usual. She'd always been a sensitive child, concerned for others, and now she'd added a maturity to it that was very attractive.

She was only a year younger than Anna. The comparison made her stomach turn over.

"So sorry I was late getting back today. I hope it didn't mess up any plans." She managed a smile.

"No, nothing at all." Janie glanced to the window. "Ach, here's Grossdaadi." She gulped down the rest of her cider. "Let's go say hi."

Benjy bolted from his seat. "I want to tie up the horse." The screen door slammed behind him.

Beth forced herself to her feet, feeling about a hundred years old. But before she could get outside, her father had come in. He caught her in a hug.

"Sit down, sit down. You look tired."

"I guess I am, a little. Do you want coffee?" She turned to the stove, but he shook his head.

"I'll have some cider. Sit down."

Taking it as an order, she sank into the chair. Daadi poured a glass for each of them.

"How did you convince Benjy not to come in with you?" she asked.

"I said he could help Janie drive the buggy up and down the lane. Don't worry about them. Janie is a good, responsible girl."

"Yah, she is. I was just thinking that." She hesitated. "You wanted to talk to me?"

Daad gave a brisk nod and brushed his hand against his full, brownish-red beard. "I looked into this business of Elijah wanting to buy into the store." He hesitated. "I don't want to speak ill of someone in the church, but I think you'd do better to look for someone else if you want to sell. He has a reputation for cutting corners and not treating his employees very well. What does Daniel think?"

Daniel's name was like a sensitive spot on her skin. She tried to collect herself. "He wants me to do whatever is best for me and Benjy. But he did make it clear that he'd hate to be partners with Elijah."

"And what about you? Do you want to sell?"

Beth thought of everything that had happened in the past weeks. She'd enjoyed working in the store, and it had given her a sense of accomplishment. Her feelings for Daniel had grown, to be honest with herself. But she wasn't sure any longer. Could she go on working with him every day? She certainly couldn't decide when she didn't know what was going to happen with Anna and the bishop.

"I don't know." She struggled for words, but before she could find any, Daad had given a brisk nod.

"Well, then, you shouldn't decide. And that's a gut way to turn Elijah down. If you do decide later, you should take your time and look at all the possibilities."

It made the most sense of anything she'd been thinking. "Denke, Daadi. I think that's what is best, too."

"That's settled, then. Do you want me to speak to Elijah for you?"

She'd love to say yes, but that probably wasn't befitting a grown woman who was partner in a business. "No, I'll take care of it. Denke."

"Gut." He stood up. "Now I will take Janie and Benjy home with me for supper, and we'll bring him back at bedtime. In the meanwhile, you have a nice rest."

She followed him, protesting. "You don't need to do that."

"We want to," he said, watching as Benjy drove the buggy back to them with Janie's hands hovering over his on the lines. "Rest now. You don't have to do everything yourself."

No, she didn't. And she was truly blessed to have such a loving family to help her.

Chapter Fifteen

Beth had thought to be at work early the next day, but by the time she'd seen Benjy off to her brother Eli's house to spend the day, she had to hurry down the lane to the store. She didn't know what her family knew or guessed, but without any questions or advice, they had rallied around.

When Daadi had brought Benjy back at supper time, he'd also brought a meal, still warm and ready to be put on the table. And with it he'd brought an invitation for Benjy to spend the day with his cousins. She had nearly cried with gratitude.

If you don't know what else to do for someone in time of trouble, you can pray and take food. That's never the wrong thing to do.

Her mother's oft-repeated advice made her smile, despite the fact that she'd assumed this day would include nothing to smile about. Her very practical mother had it right. The warm supper had comforted her, and with Benjy off having fun with his cousins today, she didn't need to fear that he'd hear something he shouldn't.

Beth shivered a little, wrapping her sweater more tightly around her. The morning breeze was colder, sweeping along the lane and stripping leaves from the trees. Autumn seemed to be passing faster than ever, or was it just that she was a year older?

And a year wiser? She thought back over the events of recent months, unsure as to whether *wiser* was the right word. Certainly she'd had her eyes opened, but it was too soon to know if she'd learned something.

Going in the back entrance, she listened for voices. The only one she heard was that of Timothy, irrepressible as always, teasing Daniel about something.

What if Anna didn't come? The bishop had responded to her call, suggesting she and Anna come between ten and twelve this morning. If he'd been curious as to what brought the two of them to seek his advice, he hadn't betrayed it in his voice.

If Anna didn't show up… Well, she didn't know what she ought to do. Shaking off the question, she hung up her sweater and bonnet and told herself to stop borrowing trouble. She had enough worries without jumping ahead to create more. Anna was probably here already, wondering where she was.

Smoothing her apron down, Beth marched from the office to the store, uttering an inarticulate prayer and hardly knowing what to pray for.

She sent a quick searching glance around the store, but she didn't find Anna. Her gaze caught Daniel's, and he shook his head at her obvious query.

Beth felt flattened and her worries came back in force. If Anna had lost her nerve, Beth would have to think of some explanation for the bishop. If she'd told her parents, she supposed that Hiram would try to exact the full penalty of the church, and the whole ugly story would become public.

With a word to Timothy, Daniel came over to her. "She hasn't come in yet, and I haven't heard from her. Have you heard anything?"

Beth shook her head. She tried to remember to treat him coolly, but she was too worried, and Daniel was the only one she could talk to.

"Not since yesterday. We can see Bishop Tom this morning between ten and twelve. If she doesn't show up, I'm not sure what to do."

Daniel touched her hand lightly—a barely felt brush of a leaf. "Try not to worry. She may well be here before then. If not, we'll figure out what to do."

She ought to resent his effort to include himself, but she couldn't help being relieved to feel she wasn't alone. "Denke." She kept her voice low, seeing Timothy approaching.

"You want me to put the Open sign up, Onkel Daniel?" His gaze slipped from one to the other of them, obviously wondering, but at least not asking what was going on.

"Yah, go ahead. Then you can take the checkout."

Timothy made a slight grimace at his uncle's directions, but he didn't say anything. When he walked off to unlock the door, Beth gave Daniel a questioning glance.

"What does he have against checking customers out?"

Daniel attempted to smile. "I think it gives less time to talk to any girls who happen to come in. What his mother would say, I don't know."

"I can certainly take it. Having something to occupy my mind will help."

"Are you sure you wouldn't rather work in the office? You can update the orders. If... When Anna shows up, I'll send her in."

Actually, that did sound better. It might be difficult to talk to customers when her mind was skittering from one thing to another like a water bug on a pond.

"All right." She hesitated, feeling as if there were something else she should say but not finding the words. Finally, she gave him a meaningless smile and hurried off to the office.

Closing the office door behind her, Beth let out a long breath. Daniel had been right. She needed four walls around her, protecting her from any curious glances.

If Anna didn't come... She slammed the question down. She'd cope with that if and when it happened. Right now, she was better off concentrating on facts and figures.

She'd made her way through one column of figures and started another when the office door creaked. Anna crept in, wrapping a shawl around her and sliding along the wall as if to remain invisible.

Beth hadn't realized how much she'd feared that Anna wouldn't show up. Relief made her feel weak for a moment.

"I'm glad you're here, Anna. Are you all right?"

Anna nodded, but her face was so sallow she looked as if she wanted to disappear into the woodwork. "The bishop?"

Beth stood. "He'll see us this morning. We should leave in about forty-five minutes." She rounded the desk and took Anna's arm. "We'll have coffee before we go. That will make you feel better."

It could hardly make her worse. At the moment she looked as if she'd pass out at an unkind word.

Putting her arm around the girl, she led her next door to the break room. Guiding her to a chair, she pushed Anna into it and started making the coffee.

This might be a little easier if they talked, but she couldn't find anything to say. The main thing between them loomed like an enormous barricade that might collapse on them at a careless word.

She'd have to find a way to talk before they reached Bishop Tom, or they'd sit there staring at each other.

Beth and Anna arrived at Bishop Thomas Braun's wheelwright workshop, with Beth relieved to see that no other buggies were pulled up in the lane. Bishop Tom's services were in demand, since wheelwrights were few and far between. She remembered her grandmother telling her once that some folks were dismayed when the lot fell on Thomas Braun, calling him to the ministry. Some had feared he wouldn't be able to do both jobs.

Somehow, like every Amish person called by God, he'd taken care of the community's spiritual needs as well as their buggies. Now that he was bishop, he had in his charge not only their church but also the adjoining one. He'd never failed to be there when his people needed him.

Swinging herself down from her buggy, Beth murmured a silent prayer that both she and Anna would be able to explain this tangled story in a way he'd understand.

When she rounded the buggy, she found that Anna was still sitting on the seat. Her head was bent, and she seemed frozen in the spot.

Beth reached up to touch her arm, fearing she'd have to push and pull the girl into the bishop's presence. "Komm now, Anna. It's time."

Anna looked at her, her eyes wide with fright and her lips trembling. She gave Beth the impression she was unable to speak.

"I know," she said softly. "But it must be done, no matter how hard it is. For either of us."

Maybe the reminder that Beth was hurting as well got through to her. With Beth's help, Anna climbed down. Grasping her arm, Beth propelled her into the long metal building.

Bishop Thomas rose from kneeling beside the wheel of a family buggy and came toward them.

"I am glad you're here," he said, his voice grave as befitted the occasion. "Komm. We'll go into my room."

The room proved to be a small frame shed attached to the workshop, containing a desk, a shelf of books and several chairs. Following his gesture, Beth led Anna to a seat and sat down next to her, feeling as apprehensive as if waiting for a scolding from Mamm for some childish mischief. But there was nothing childish about this.

"Now we can talk. No one will disturb us." He looked from one to the other, his blue eyes keen and kind.

With his long beard, grown gray in his service to his people, he'd always reminded Beth of an Old Testament prophet—one of the stern but forgiving ones.

Beth realized that Anna was frozen again. Apparently, she'd have to go first. Maybe that was the best thing— she could unravel the story as it had occurred to her.

"I'm afraid it's a long story." She glanced uncertainly at Anna. "I'll have to start at the beginning."

He nodded. "Take as long as you need."

A deep breath seemed to give her the courage she needed. "It started when Lydia, my cousin, and I were getting James's clothes ready to give away. I hadn't touched anything until about a month after his passing."

She stopped for breath. At least she'd started. There was no turning back now. "In a drawer under his clothing, I found a note. It was obviously from a woman, and it pleaded with James to meet her at the usual place."

Bishop Tom's eyes twitched at that, and he glanced toward Anna.

"At first I didn't know what to think. I was angry and hurt, and I kept thinking I must find out who it was." She paused, trying to think how to put it. "I was hurt and angry with both of them. I couldn't think of anything else. But I kept trying to pray about it, and as time went on, I knew I couldn't keep living in the past. It wasn't gut for me or for Benjy. Then this week, I found out." She looked at Anna. "She confessed to me, and she asked for my forgiveness."

She came to a stop, not knowing what else to say. It was Anna's turn now.

Bishop Tom looked from her to Anna, who seemed to shrink under his gaze. "Anna?"

Her face twisted as she struggled to speak. "I was the one. I didn't mean to do anything wrong. I was so unhappy, and James was kind. He was always smiling, and when he smiled at me, I felt better."

"So you met with him. Did you sneak out to do this?"

Anna sniffled and nodded.

"How many times?"

Was he counting up Anna's sins? Maybe they had to admit each wrong in order to be forgiven. How many sins did *she* have on her conscience?

"F-four," Anna whispered. "At that old schoolhouse on Owl Hollow Road."

He was still for a moment. When he spoke, his voice was grave. "I must ask you, Anna. How far did this relationship with James go?"

Anna was crying now, tears flowing freely, and Beth felt her eyes sting with tears.

"We just talked mostly," she whispered. "Sometimes he hugged me. Twice he…he kissed me." The whisper had gone almost to silence.

When she looked at the bishop again, Beth had the sense that he'd aged in the past few minutes. It was as if he'd taken their wrongs upon himself.

"And that's all?"

Anna nodded, sobbing.

"Do you wish to confess your sins and be restored to a right relationship with God and His people?"

"Yah." Her voice was choked with sobs, but she seemed to sense that she had to say this aloud.

Bishop Thomas turned his gaze to her, and Beth felt as if he could see right through her.

"Beth, have you forgiven Anna for the wrong she has done to you?"

"Yah." She couldn't say it fast enough. How could she blame that miserable child for what had happened? It was James who would be difficult to forgive.

"Have you forgiven James for breaking his wedding vows?" He seemed to read her mind.

"I am trying." She wiped away tears. "I say I forgive him, but I have to do it again." She looked at him. "But I am trying."

He nodded, as if satisfied. "Do you wish to confess whatever lack of forgiveness is still in your heart and be restored to a right relationship with God?"

"Yah." She wiped the tears again. "I do."

He glanced from one to the other. "Please kneel and confess."

Anna was almost on her knees already, but she sank the rest of the way. Beth, slipping to her knees, watched Anna warily, half-afraid she would pass out.

But she began, managing in a shaking voice to confess her wrongs and ask for forgiveness.

Then it was Beth's turn. Confessing her initial anger was easy enough, as was declaring her forgiveness of Anna. The challenge was asking with a whole heart to be able to forgive James.

When it was done and forgiveness proclaimed, a cleansing warmth swept through her. It was in the past, forgiven. No one else ever needed to know. She turned to Anna, and in a moment they were in each other's arms, weeping but rejoicing.

Daniel had managed to spend most of the day within sight of the windows, watching for any sign of Beth's buggy. Finally, at midafternoon, it came in view, but she didn't stop at the store. She drove straight down the lane toward her own house.

He fought down his disappointment. He'd expected that at least she'd tell him what had happened. Maybe she felt he'd forfeited any right to feel concern for her.

Since she was alone, he'd guess she'd taken Anna on home. How would that have gone? If Anna had to tell her parents the whole story, that would have been an unpleasant time, to say the least. For the Fisher family, for sure, but for Beth, as well.

He rubbed the back of his neck, feeling the taut muscles react painfully to the touch. He told himself he'd done the right thing for both Beth and Anna, but that was small comfort given Beth's feelings.

When Timothy left, Daniel locked the front door and pulled down the shades. On any ordinary day, he'd check out and then go home, where Mamm and his sister-in-law would have supper ready. Today he'd choke if he tried to eat.

They wouldn't worry if he didn't show up. They'd just put something back for him, assuming something had detained him at the store. He was detained, all right, but not in the way they'd think. And there was always something to do here.

Daniel was checking inventory in the storeroom when he heard the rattle of the front doorknob. If it was a belated customer wanting him to open up, he or she would have to do without.

Before he could argue with himself about it, he heard another sound—a key turning in the lock and the door opening. Beth? His heart jumped into his throat, and his fingers slid from the shelf.

Cautious, half-afraid of how she'd look and what she'd say, he opened the door a few inches and stood watching her.

Beth wasn't looking in his direction. Did she think the store was empty? She walked slowly back through the store, pausing to look from one thing to another, reaching out to touch a shelf or straighten a carton.

It was almost as if she were saying goodbye, and his heart sank. He could hardly expect anything else. If she thought he'd deceived her, she wouldn't want to work with him any longer.

She turned slightly, and he got a better look at her face. It was pale and drained, and yet she didn't look shaken. She looked at peace, as if she'd accepted whatever happened with the bishop as God's will.

He must have made some sound, because Beth glanced toward the back of the store and saw him. He held his breath, wondering if he'd know what she was thinking when she spoke.

"Daniel. I thought you'd left."

He shook his head. "I couldn't. Not when I was worrying about what happened to you. Did Bishop Thomas agree with the way you wanted to handle it?"

For a moment, she looked as if she didn't know what he was talking about. Then she seemed to realize. "Yah. Well, actually, I never had a chance to ask it. He listened to both of us, and he was so kind, so understanding." Her face relaxed in a half smile. "Once Bishop Thomas took over, I guess I realized that it was foolish to try to tell him what to do."

That was good, he guessed. He'd never had to confess anything of that sort, but he thought a great deal of the bishop's wisdom and his knowledge of his people.

"What about Anna?" He moved a little closer to her, alert for any sign that she found it intrusive.

"I was afraid once or twice that she'd pass out. But other than that, she was all right. She held herself together and told the whole story, just the way she'd told it to me."

"Gut." He began to relax a little. If the truth was out to the bishop, surely there was not much to worry about. "I'm glad. I was afraid she'd fall to pieces and not be able to tell him."

Her old smile lit her face. "Me, too. I've never been so glad. I didn't have to try and explain it."

Daniel was so relieved to see the old Beth again that he wanted to laugh. "No public confession?"

Beth shook her head. "Bishop Thomas listened to her confession and announced her forgiveness. And then he asked me to confess."

"Wh-what did you have to confess? You were the injured party."

"He asked if I had forgiven Anna. And then he asked if I'd forgiven James."

"That would be harder."

"Yah. I could only say I was trying. And I'd keep on trying." Her voice shook a little. "Sometimes I think I have, and then it jumps back up again."

She was struggling, and he longed to help her but didn't know how. "That is natural, isn't it? When someone has hurt you so badly?"

Beth nodded, giving him a look of gratitude, her eyes filled with tears, so that they looked more than ever like two green lakes. He couldn't help it—he took both her hands in his. She didn't pull away.

"I think I understand James better now," she said. "Or maybe I see him more clearly. He had faults and weaknesses like we all do, but he wasn't a bad person."

Daniel thought of his friend as a boy, as a teenager and then as the man he'd become. He'd been self-centered at times, spoiled, maybe, but Daniel couldn't regret their friendship.

"Yah, you're right."

"For a time, I thought that I could never trust anyone again." She went on, her voice as soft as if she spoke to herself. "But that was so foolish. There were people I already trusted, even when I told myself that. People like Daad and Mamm. And you."

He was sure he'd heard only what he'd wished. But she was looking at him, her eyes clear and untroubled. He felt her pulse beating against his hands, and he knew that what he'd always wanted was within reach.

It was too soon, of course. They both knew that. But he had to speak. Even if they had to wait, it would be worth it.

He moved his fingers caressingly on the soft skin on the inside of her wrists. "Once, a long time ago, I realized that it was you I wanted, but I let James edge me out of the picture. I won't do that again."

A smile trembled on her lips as she lifted her face to his. "No. Please don't do that again."

Carefully he drew her closer, until she rested against him and their lips met once, very lightly. "I love you, Beth. When it's time, I want to marry you. To be Benjy's father and maybe the father of other kinder with you. And I will cherish you all my life."

They stood close together, hands clasped, and he knew that out of the shattered remains of marriage and friendship had come a love that was stronger—one that would last a lifetime in obedience to God.

* * * * *

*If you enjoyed this story,
don't miss the previous books in the
Brides of Lost Creek series from Marta Perry:*

Second Chance Amish Bride
The Wedding Quilt Bride
The Promised Amish Bride

Find more great reads at www.LoveInspired.com

Dear Reader,

Welcome back to Lost Creek, where we'll meet three cousins who are devoted to each other and stand by one another whatever befalls them. With faith and love, Beth, Lydia and Miriam face the future with courage, always holding their family ties close even as they search for a love that will last a lifetime.

I hope that you'll enjoy my story and come back again for another visit to the Amish community of Lost Creek. Please let me know how you feel about this new book. You can reach me at marta@martaperry.com, at www.martaperry.com and at www.Facebook.com/martaperrybooks.

If you send me your mailing address, I'll be happy to send you a Marta Perry bookmark and my brochure of Pennsylvania Dutch recipes.

Blessings,

Marta Perry

SPECIAL EXCERPT FROM

LOVE INSPIRED
INSPIRATIONAL ROMANCE

Can the new teacher in this Amish community help the family next door without losing her heart?

Read on for a sneak preview of
The Amish Teacher's Dilemma *by Patricia Davids,*
available in March 2020 from Love Inspired.

Clang, clang, clang.

The hammering outside her new schoolhouse grew louder. Eva Coblentz moved to the window to locate the source of the clatter. Across the road she saw a man pounding on an ancient-looking piece of machinery with steel wheels and a scoop-like nose on the front end.

When he had the sheet of metal shaped to fit the front of the machine, he stood back to assess his work. He knelt and hammered on the shovel-like nose three more times. Satisfied, he gathered up his tools and started in her direction.

She stepped back from the window. Was he coming to the school? Why? Had he noticed her gawking? Perhaps he only wanted to welcome the new teacher, although his lack of a beard said he wasn't married.

She glanced around the room. Should she meet him by the door? That seemed too eager. Her eyes settled on the large desk at the front of the classroom. She should look as if she was ready for the school year to start. A professional attitude would put off any suggestion that she was interested in meeting single men.

LIEXP0220

Eva hurried to the desk, pulled out the chair and sat down as the outside door opened. The chair tipped over backward, sending her flailing. Her head hit the wall with a painful thud as she slid to the floor. Stunned, she slowly opened her eyes to see the man leaning over the desk.

He had the most beautiful gray eyes she'd ever beheld. They were rimmed with thick, dark lashes in stark contrast to the mop of curly, dark red hair springing out from beneath his straw hat. Tiny sparks of light whirled around him.

"I'm Willis Gingrich. Local blacksmith." He squatted beside her. "Can you tell me your name?"

The warmth and strength of his hand on her skin sent a sizzle of awareness along her nerve endings. "I'm Eva Coblentz. I am the new teacher and I'm fine now."

Don't miss
The Amish Teacher's Dilemma
by USA TODAY *bestselling author Patricia Davids,*
available March 2020 wherever
Love Inspired books and ebooks are sold.

LoveInspired.com